She glanced up at him quickly, surprised at the mockery in his voice. 'I thought this was a busy practice with a dedicated staff but you make them sound rather—well —immature.'

'Oh, we're dedicated all right and very hard working,' he frowned, 'immature? Yes, perhaps. They're all rather young—' he looked at her quizzically, 'about your age. I'm the oldest, therefore the most disillusioned. I don't judge a book by its cover.'

'How very wise.' Determined not to be put down by his cynical attitude, she turned to study him openly.

He was wildly handsome with dark, unruly hair falling across his forehead and even darker eyebrows. His mouth was firm and his chin was strong and determined. It was a stormy face on the whole, modified to some degree by an undoubtedly attractive smile reflected in those brilliant eyes.

He stood still, smiling a little grimly under her critical inspection then he said calmly, 'Yes. I'm thirty-four. Long past the calf love stage. Women are pleasant diversions but my work comes first.'

Mary Bowring was born in Suffolk. She went to a convent school in Belgium and joined the Women's Auxiliary Air Force in the Second World War, during which time she met and married her husband who was in the Army. She took up writing after the birth of a son and daughter and published three books about her life as a veterinary surgeon's wife. *Vets in Love* is her second Doctor Nurse Romance, following *Village Vet*.

VETS IN LOVE

BY

MARY BOWRING

MILLS & BOON LIMITED
ETON HOUSE   18-24 PARADISE ROAD
RICHMOND   SURREY   TW9 1SR

First published in Great Britain 1988
by Mills & Boon Limited

© Mary Bowring 1988

Australian copyright 1988
Philippine copyright 1988
This edition 1988

ISBN 0 263 76178 9

Set in Baskerville 10 on 10½ pt.
03 – 8810 – 57272

Typeset in Great Britain by JCL Graphics, Bristol

Made and Printed in Great Britain

CHAPTER ONE

JOANNA BRAMFORD turned her car into the space beside
the door marked Veterinary Surgery and gave a sigh of
relief. It had been a long drive from East Anglia to this
Sussex market town, and she sat for a few moments trying
to relax before going in to announce her arrival.

Idly she took stock of her surroundings, the block of
surgery buildings and the large red house across the yard
where she had been told the junior partner lived. She had
been here once before when she had been interviewed by
Mr Mayfield, the senior partner in this veterinary
practice. He had shown her round the surgery,
introduced her to his partner and, a week later she had
received a letter offering her the post for which she had
applied—veterinary surgeon in charge of the small animal
section. Just the job she wanted, great for experience and
a long way from the Suffolk town where she had worked
since qualifying a year ago. A year that had begun so full
of hope and ended so tragically that, even now, she could
not look back without feeling a sharp stab of anguish.

Shaking off the sudden chill of remembrance, she
opened the car door and stood for a moment searching for
a way into the house where she had been told to report.

Suddenly a door in the wall opened and a man came
through and walked towards the surgery buildings. A tall,
broad, dark-haired man of about thirty who glanced at
her curiously as she went up to him. His eyes, almost
silver-grey under black brows, swept over her in
unconcealed admiration as she asked smilingly,

'Excuse me—is that the way in to Mr Holman's house?
I've been told to report there.'

'Yes. It's the side entrance——' He paused. 'Are you—why, of course, you must be the new vet.'

She nodded, 'Joanna Bramford,' and took his outstretched hand. 'How do you do?'

'Welcome to the practice. I'm Paul Copeland.' He continued to hold her hand. 'I missed you when you came for your interview, but I can see that the reports I heard, glowing though they were, didn't do justice to you.'

She laughed. 'What on earth do you mean?'

He gave her another long, appraising look. 'Well, you're quite devastatingly beautiful. Your hair—cloudy and dark—dark blue eyes—lovely curling mouth, and your figure—wow!' He paused, his mouth twitching at the corner as she stiffened rather resentfully. 'You're going to cause havoc among my male colleagues'. Joanna pulled her hand away and gazed back at him coolly. 'Really? Well, let's hope they won't be as susceptible as you seem to be think, Mr Copeland.' She turned towards the door in the wall. 'I must go and announce myself to Mrs Holman.'

He moved swiftly and opened the door. 'I'll come with you. Mrs Holman is in the kitchen. She's a kind of mother figure in the practice—hands out coffee and tea at all hours and listens to our troubles. The veterinary nurses weep on her shoulder when their love affairs go wrong.'

She glanced up at him quickly, surprised at the mockery in his voice. 'I thought this was a busy practice with a dedicated staff, but you make them sound rather—well, immature.'

'Oh, we're dedicated all right and very hard-working.' He frowned. 'Immature? Yes, perhaps. They're all rather young—' he looked at her quizzically, 'about your age. I'm the oldest, therefore the most disillusioned. I don't judge a book by its cover.'

'How very wise.' Determined not to be put down by his cynical attitude, Joanna turned to study him openly.

He was wildly handsome, with dark, unruly hair falling

across his forehead and even darker eyebrows. His mouth was firm and his chin was strong and determined. It was a stormy face on the whole, modified to some degree by an undoubtedly attractive smile reflected in those brilliant eyes.

He stood still, smiling a little grimly under her critical inspection, then he said calmly, 'Yes. I'm thirty-four, long past the calf love stage. Women are pleasant diversions, but my work comes first.'

She nodded and said lightly, 'I feel the same way about men. I've come here to widen my experience, and that's the only thing I'm interested in.' She paused and reached out to knock at the door. 'No need for you to waste any more time, I can introduce myself.'

He turned the handle. 'Mrs Holman doesn't stand on ceremony,' he said smoothly.

His words were borne out by the warm welcome extended by the pretty, middle-aged woman who looked up smilingly from an ironing board. A large pile of folded garments stood on a side table and a basketful yet to be done was quickly pushed aside.

Soon they were sipping hot tea and dipping into a tin of biscuits, and it took only a few minutes for Joanna to realise that Paul Copeland's description of Mrs Holman as a mother figure was the only possible way in which to describe her. In the pleasant atmosphere of the kitchen and the totally unpretentious attitude of the junior partner's wife Joanna relaxed and began to lose all the tension she had felt during her long drive towards her new way of life. She felt even more at ease when, after refusing a second cup of tea, Paul got up and with a quick word of thanks left the two women alone.

'I'll take you over to your flat soon,' said Mrs Holman. 'You'll have the weekend to yourself and then, on Monday, the small animal surgery will be all yours.'

Joanna thought for a moment, then asked tentatively, 'Mr Mayfield said there are two veterinary nurses—are they both on duty at once?'

'Not at the moment. Part-time—one in the morning and one in the afternoon, but they're always willing to put in extra time if necessary.'

'What are they like? I mean—' Joanna hesitated, 'I'm sure they're good at their work, but—well, are they easy to get on with?'

Mrs Holman smiled. 'Oh, yes. They're really nice girls. A bit scatty at times with their various boyfriends, but I keep my eyes on them and hand out advice like a Dutch uncle—aunt.'

Remembering what Paul Copeland had said, Joanna laughed. 'And the vets? There are several assistants, aren't there?'

Mrs Holman nodded. 'There's Sandy Wilson—mad on exercise and keeping fit. Apt to turn cartwheels and tends to show off a bit when we have a party. Then there's Mark Pritchard—very serious but kind and understanding and Paul Copeland whom you've already met.'

'Four assistants now, with me.' Joanna looked thoughtful.

'Ah, but I forgot—Sandy is leaving soon. He's taking up a post in the Ministry of Agriculture, and Paul—well, I rather think he won't be here much longer. He wants to set up on his own. He's a brilliant vet and we'll be very sorry to lose him. We've tried to persuade him to stay—offered a partnership, but—' Mrs Holman shrugged ruefully, 'well, there it is.' She paused. 'You've met my husband—he's more or less in charge of everything down here because Mr Mayfield only does consultancies—horses. All over the country—he's a great horse expert. His daughter Clare works in the office—a pretty girl, though not—' Mrs Holman paused, 'well, she's not popular with everybody.'

'Goodness!' Joanna's eyes widened. 'I feel a bit dazed. So many people—the practice is larger than I thought.'

'Is it? Actually it's only what I should call a medium size practice. Some of them are like small empires, with branch surgeries all around. Even so, some of our assistants say it's too big and grumble occasionally when they can't see their cases through. But that's usually Clare's fault. She passes on messages rather too carelessly. She's inclined to—well, she's the senior partner's daughter and well aware of it.' Mrs Holman laughed. 'I'm talking too much as usual! One of my many failings. Anyway, I hope you'll soon settle in here. If you have any problems that I can help you solve I'm always available.'

Joanna smiled gratefully. 'Yes, Paul Copeland said you were—well, everybody's friend. That's nice to know.'

'I try to be.' Mrs Holman smiled ruefully. 'In a practice like this there are bound to be a few personality clashes.' She paused. 'What did you think of Paul?'

Joanna hesitated. 'Difficult to say. I don't think we hit it off very well. He seemed—oh, I don't know. He's probably all right when you get to know him. Is he married?'

Immediately after posing the question Joanna regretted having asked, but Mrs Holman didn't seem to find her curiosity unusual.

She shook her head. 'No, but it's not for lack of opportunity. He goes out with lots of girls, but there doesn't seem to be anyone in particular. He told me once that he'd never met a girl he couldn't live without.'

'That's a bit arrogant,' Joanna said sharply, but Mrs Holman shook her head again.

'No, I think he's right to take his time. He's terribly good-looking and the girls fall for him so quickly that he's bound to be a bit wary.'

Joanna said nothing but made a mental resolve not to follow the herd. Paul Copeland might have the reputation of a heartbreaker, but her own heart had suffered already, and once was enough.

Mrs Holman rose to her feet. 'Let's go over to your flat. I gather you saw it when you came for your interview, but if there's anything extra you need you have only to ask.'

The flat, which was situated over the small animal surgery, was very pleasant—a good-sized living room, small kitchen well fitted up, two bedrooms, one large and the other just big enough to accommodate a guest—it was comfortably furnished and recently decorated. While Joanna was unpacking she wondered rather nervously whether she would find it difficult to adjust to this new way of life. Since qualifying she had worked as assistant in a practice near her parents' home. She and her elderly employer, with one veterinary nurse, had dealt with a variety of patients, but the practice was nothing like as busy as this new one promised to be. Mrs Holman had hinted at occasional differences between members of staff, but that would hardly affect her personally as she was gong to be in sole charge of the small animal side. In any case, she was determined to keep herself to herself. She would be friendly but reserved. Gradually she would build up some kind of social life outside the practice—work and pleasure, she had found to her cost, were best kept apart.

As she arranged her books on the shelves in the living room a sudden feeling of desolation threatened to overwhelm her. She had been so happy in Suffolk—so much in love with James. James, who had walked into the surgery one day with his Labrador and, from that first encounter, had changed her whole life. Now, sad and disillusioned, she was forced to work with strangers in order to escape the cruel gossip against which she had had no defence.

For a few moments longer she gazed unseeingly at her books, then quickly, impatiently she turned away. It was no use bemoaning the past. She had learnt a bitter lesson—a lesson that she would remember all her life.

Glancing at her watch, she saw that there was just time

for a bath before taking up Mrs Holman's invitation to supper. It was a very pleasant meal and Mr Holman, a gentle, courteous man, was full of interesting anecdotes derived from his many years of experience as a vet in a mixed practice. It was while they were having coffee that he suggested Joanna should look in at the small animal surgery next morning in order to familiarise herself with the equipment, some of which might be new to her.

'It might save you getting flustered on Monday morning,' he said, 'because what with one thing and another things are a bit chaotic at the moment. Clare Mayfield is working in your office, and she also takes the telephone messages.'

Joanna looked surprised. 'I thought the small animal section was completely self-contained.'

'It's only a temporary measure.' Mr Holman looked rather embarrassed. 'The general reception office next door is being re-roofed, so Clare has had to move in with you and share the telephone.'

'Not much sharing about it—she rules the roost,' said Mrs Holman drily. 'Still, it's only for a few weeks.'

Joanna nodded and managed to hide the uneasy suspicion that was taking root in her mind. From the hints that Mrs Holman had let fall it seemed that the daughter of the senior partner was inclined to throw her weight around. Well, just so long as she didn't interfere in the veterinary work everything would probably be all right.

Next morning, after an early breakfast, she decided to take Mr Holman's advice. Surgery began, she knew, at nine o'clock and, with half an hour in hand, she could study the equipment and see where the drugs were kept. Taking the key she had been given, she went down the stairs from her flat and entered the surgery from the back door.

From the waiting room she went into the consulting/examination room and stood for a moment admiring the layout. The fittings and overall décor were very pleasing. Spotless of course, and completely up to date. A surgery to inspire confidence in a nervous client. A sudden noise from what was obviously the dispensary behind her made her go to investigate and, to her surprise, she saw Paul Copeland searching along the shelf of veterinary drugs.

He turned and smiled. 'Hello—come to survey your future territory?'

She nodded. 'I thought I'd better do a bit of reconnaissance. Some of this equipment looks rather awe-inspiring.'

'Let me show you round—plenty of time before surgery begins. Sandy Wilson is doing it this morning. We've been doing it in turns since Jean Russell left.' He laughed. 'I admit, though, I'm very glad to get back to my large animals.'

'Don't you like small animal work?'

He shrugged. 'It's not the work—I like it all. What I don't like is being cooped up most of the day indoors. I much prefer to get out into the country—the farms and villages.' He paused. 'Jean Russell used to get a bit fed-up too—especially in the summer. Sometimes on her day off she'd go out with one of us on our calls. Would you like to do that? You're very welcome to come with me.' Then, suddenly, his eyes gleamed with sardonic amusement. 'No, I don't suppose you would, though. You'll have too many social engagements.'

'What makes you think that?' His mocking tone irritated her. 'I don't know anyone in this area.'

'Ah, but it won't be long before you do. You'll soon have all the eligible and probably also the ineligible males round you like bees round a honeypot.'

'For heaven's sake!' Joanna frowned angrily. 'Stop treating me like a—a sex object! I'm a vet and I've come here to work. The sooner you get that firmly fixed in your mind the better.'

He blinked in pretended alarm and put up his hands as

though to ward off her attack. 'OK, OK! No need to fly off the handle. I get the message.' He paused. 'Why do you find this equipment awe-inspiring?'

'Well the practice in Suffolk where I worked was run by an elderly vet. A very good vet too, but his equipment was nothing like as modern as it is here. That anaesthetic machine, for istance—it looks highly complicated.'

'Not really. You'll soon get used to it. In any case, Liz and Chrissie, the two veterinary nurses, are very competent. No need to worry while you're operating—they'll have everything under control. Now, in that corner the record cards are filed. The nurse on duty will produce the appropriate card as soon as an owner with a patient arrives. In the dispensary over there we've got all the drugs and there's a refrigerator for vaccines. The examination table is an electrically operated raise-and-lower one and the operating table is adjustable. That room over there is the office—the communication centre with telephone, appointments book, post tray and, of course, the all-important radio telephone link to each vet's car.' He stopped, then indicating the office door, he added, 'Now that is the cause of a lot of trouble. Clare Mayfield is really only the receptionist and usually works in the general reception office next door, but that building is being repaired. She shouldn't really affect you at all—her job is dealing with large animal clients and passing on the messages to vets working on farms or stables or whatever. Unfortunately she's created quite a lot of bad feeling in this surgery by taking over the small animal messages and making appointments. She's not terribly efficient even at her own job, and she's even more useless here.'

Joanna frowned. 'I gathered as much from Mrs Holman. Why on earth is she allowed to get away with it?'

Paul shrugged. 'Nepotism—Mr Mayfield's only daughter. Her fond parents are quite blind to her lack of ability.'

'But that's ridiculous! A big practice like this and she's allowed to mess things up. Why don't you all protest?'

Paul smiled wryly. 'Do you suppose we haven't tried? That was one of the main reasons for Jean Russell leaving. And she'll be followed by others. Sandy Wilson is seeking refuge in the Min of Ag and even Mark Pritchard, usually quite unflappable, is getting restless.'

Joanna eyed him curiously. 'Mrs Holman said she thought you too—' she paused, 'well, she said she thought you'd eventually set up on your own.'

He nodded. 'I've always meant to do that. I don't like working in a large practice. I'll probably go back to Suffolk.' He stopped and looked at her questioningly. 'Suffolk—why, of course, that's where you've come from. That's interesting. Whereabouts?'

'Burton, just north of Ipswich. I worked in Mr Bridges' practice.'

'Good lord!' He stood gazing at her in surprise. 'I know him. I was born in Ipswich—my father was a doctor there. He's dead now, unfortunately, and so is my mother, but I still go back there when I have a weekend off to see my sister who lives in the country. How strange that we've never met. My sister takes her dogs to Mr Bridges.' He smiled. 'When I'm home, of course, she calls on me, though, families being what they are, I think she has more faith in old Bridges.' He laughed suddenly. 'Talking like this of Suffolk makes me quite home sick! I can't wait to get back. There's something about East Anglia——' he stopped and glanced at her curiously. 'How on earth could you bring yourself to leave? Weren't you happy there?'

Joanna stiffened, then said guardedly, 'It was a—a personal matter.'

Paul smiled a little cynically. 'A man, I suppose. Not Mr Bridges of course, he's old enough to be your father, but I'll bet——'

She flushed resentfully. 'Just confine your bets to the race

course, Mr Copeland, and stop speculating about my reason
for leaving Suffolk.'

His dark eyebrows rose in mock astonishment. 'Oh, dear!
What a reaction to a joking supposition on my part! And, by
the way, we're all on Christian name terms here, or will you
insist on being called Miss Bramford?'

Angry at being ridiculed, she said coldly, 'Of course not.
Anyway, I must go. It's getting on for surgery time and I
can hear a car—probably a client.'

'More likely Sandy,' he said calmly, then following her to
the door, he added, 'As we have a common interest in
Suffolk how about coming out to dinner with me one
evening this week when we're both off duty?'

Joanna caught her breath in momentary alarm. The last
thing she wanted to do was to talk about her life in Suffolk.
Then Mrs Holman's words came echoing in her mind.
'Goes out with lots of girls,' and she found the answer to her
predicament.

'I really have very little interest in Suffolk,' she said
coolly, 'but thank you all the same for asking me. I'm sure
you must have much more in common with the other girls
here.'

Seeing the quick flare of anger in his eyes she felt a small
pang of regret at having rebuffed him, and as she made her
way upstairs to her flat, she reflected ruefully on the bad luck
which seemed to follow her. To come all this way to work
and then find someone who knew that little corner of the
country so well—it was just too bad. She would have to keep
Paul Copeland very much at a distance in future so that by
the time he next went home he would have lost interest in
her.

She spent the weekend arranging her flat and exploring
the countryside, then on Monday morning she awoke with a
slight feeling of nervousness at the prospect before her. She
dressed quickly, sweeping her hair high on her head, fixing it
with small combs and brushing the light feathery fringes to
one side; it was not practical to have it falling round her face

when examining animals on the surgery table. Surveying herself critically in the mirror, she smoothed down her delicately arched brows and decided against touching up the dark eyelashes that were so long and thick that they cast shadows on her cheeks. Pulling on her surgical overall, she went downstairs.

A veterinary nurse, tall with dark curly hair and smiling blue eyes, greeted her cheerfully. 'I'm Elizabeth Harper—Liz to everyone here,' she announced. 'I do the morning surgery with you, and Chrissie Blake comes in after lunch. We also look after the patients in the hospital and generally turn our hands to everything.'

'It sounds a good arrangement,' said Joanna. 'Who does the office work?'

'Ah, that's a debatable point,' Liz laughed. 'There was a secretary who came in three days a week, but she left just before Jean Russell and Mr Mayfield is trying to get another—so far without any success. Meantime his daughter Clare has taken it on.' She shrugged. 'She's not really up to it—gets into the most awful muddles, and we—that's Chrissie and I and most probably you now—get roped in to help her out.' She paused, then added ruefully, 'She's the fly in the ointment here, as you'll probably very soon find out.'

Joanna frowned. 'I almost begin to pity the poor girl. Everyone seems to be against her.'

'Well—' Liz looked thoughtful, 'maybe we're a bit hard on her now, but we weren't at first. It's just that she's made herself so objectionable. Anyway, you'll be able to judge for yourself soon. She's due in about nine o'clock, but she's always late.' She stopped as the sound of barking came from the waiting room. 'Here we go. Your first patient.'

A large, overweight Labrador pulled its equally large mistress into the consulting room, and Liz said cheerfully,

'Hello, Mrs Robinson. This is Miss Bramford who's come to take Miss Russell's place.' Going to the filing cabinet and drawing out a card, she handed it to Joanna. 'This is Bella's case history.'

While Liz lowered the table and got the Labrador ready to be examined, Joanna studied the card carefully, then putting it aside, she began her own investigation.

Suddenly Mrs Robinson said, 'I really don't want her to be operated on, but Miss Russell said it would have to be done eventually. I'm rather hoping you'll find it won't be necessary.'

Joanna said nothing for a few moments, then she looked up. 'I'm afraid Miss Russell was right. There's a polypus on the cervix. It's not causing much trouble at the moment but, when it gets bigger, it will have to be taken away. Meantime I'd like Bella to lose quite a bit of weight.'

Mrs Robinson frowned resentfully. 'You're all the same, you vets! Miss Russell wanted me to put Bella on a diet, but it seems so cruel to me. She's never been starved in her life, and it's bad enough having to be operated on without being deprived of all her favourite foods.'

Joanna drew a long breath. 'I expect Miss Russell explained why it was necessary, and I can only repeat what she probably said. No operation is without risk and, in Bella's case, all that extra fat puts strain on her heart, to say nothing of making the actual surgery more difficult.' She stroked the bitch thoughtfully, then added, 'Bella is a beautiful, gentle animal and I can understand how difficult it is for you to refuse her anything. On the other hand, I'm sure you would want to help her make a good recovery, and you'll be doing just that if you follow my directions. I'll give you the name of an obesity diet and you can buy it in tins. Stick to that entirely for a month and she'll be in much better condition for the operation.'

Mrs Robinson gazed at Joanna for a long, thoughtful moment. Then reluctantly, she nodded. 'When you put it like that I can see that the best way of showing my love for Bella is to follow your advice.'

When she had gone Liz looked at Joanna with respect. 'Nice work,' she said quietly. 'Jean Russell never managed to convince that lady. One up to you!'

Joanna smiled pensively. So that was how it was. For the next few weeks she was going to be compared with her predecessor. It was, she supposed, inevitable, but she was bound to slip up some time. After all, Miss Russell had had many years of experience.

The patients arrived in quick succession—dogs and cats needing injections, treatment for skin diseases, wounds to be sutured and appointments made for future operations. Here it was that Joanna came up against a difficulty.

'This tumour must be removed as soon as possible.' She looked up from examining an elderly spaniel and spoke to its anxious owner. 'Tomorrow at about eleven o'clock, if that's all right with you.' She turned to Liz as the client nodded agreement. 'Well you make a note of that, please?'

Liz hesitated, then drew Joanna aside. 'All appointments have to be made through Clare. She keeps the list and she's got several things booked for tomorrow. You'll have to wait till she gets in—she's locked the book away.'

Unable to show anger in front of a client, Joanna took his telephone number and promised to ring and fix up the time for his appointment, then, as the door closed behind him, she said furiously,

'What an absurd arrangement! Why should Clare Mayfield control the appointment system, especially where ops are concerned?'

'I don't know,' Liz looked unhappy, 'but that's how it is. Her father has given her a free hand. Originally she was employed just as receptionist, but gradually——'

'Well, I'm not going to stand for it,' Joanna said firmly. 'She's not a vet or a veterinary nurse. She doesn't know which cases are urgent.' She paused, then added, 'Didn't Jean Russell complain?'

'Yes,' Liz nodded, 'she told Mr Holman and he said he'd have a word with Clare. When he did, she argued the toss and he gave in.'

'Good lord, and he's a partner—what an extraordinary situation! I think——'

Joanna broke off as the side door opened and Paul Copeland came in, followed by a younger man with a rather melancholy face.

'Where the hell is Clare?' Paul said angrily. 'We want the list of calls she took yesterday. I've got two follow-up cases to do first, then I want to organise my day.'

'Me too.' The other man came forward. 'Hello—I'm Mark Pritchard and you, I know, are Joanna Bramford. How are you coping with this idiotic set-up?'

Taken aback by this sudden invasion of her surgery, Joanna smiled and shrugged. 'It is rather strange,' she said evasively, then, as the door opened again, she stared hard at the girl who came languidly into the room. She was tall, slim with long blonde hair and hard blue eyes, but her looks were spoilt by a sulky mouth. She gazed around disdainfully, then, ignoring everybody, she went into the office.

Paul, muttering something under his breath, followed her in and shut the door behind him.

For a moment Joanna was nonplussed, then she turned to Liz. 'See if there's anyone in the waiting room, will you, please?' She smiled at Mark Pritchard. 'Excuse me, won't you? I must get on with my work.'

'Of course.' He hesitated and ran a hand through his fair hair. 'Mind if I wait here? I want to speak to Clare when Paul has finished.'

Joanna smiled wryly. 'This is a bit like a madhouse, isn't it?'

He shrugged. 'You're dead right. Something's got to be done soon or we, the assistants, will leave en masse.'

Joanna frowned to herself as Liz ushered in an anxious-looking woman with an old dog of indeterminate breed. She was engrossed in giving it a thorough examination when the sound of raised voices came from the office, causing the client to turn round in surprise. A moment later Paul came out, his face dark with anger, and stood for a moment as though wishing to speak to her. Looking up, she shook her head coldly. 'Now now, please. I'm busy.'

'Sorry. I'll wait in the store room—I want to ask you something.' He turned to Mark Pritchard. 'I've had my say and she's furious. You'd better go and add fuel to the fire.'

Mark hesitated. 'Well, if you've done your stuff perhaps I needn't——'

'Oh, for God's sake, go on,' Paul said impatiently. 'We've got to sort this out once and for all.'

Joanna glanced at her client's astonished face, then turned to glare at the two men. In a low voice she said, 'Will you please stop distracting me and settle your business elsewhere.'

With a muttered apology Mark went quickly into the office, and Paul said smoothly to the dog's owner, 'Please forgive us. There's a bit of a crisis on at the moment.'

He went into the store room and Joanna, frowning, returned to her examination. Working in a practice full of angry vets was the last thing she had anticipated, and her heart sank at the prospect of becoming involved. Clare Mayfield had not even bothered to notice her so far and her haughty manner boded ill for the future.

'Do you think my old Georgie has come to the end of the road?' The owner's voice trembled a little and Joanna, ashamed of her momentary distraction, looked up smilingly, glad to be able to reassure her.

'Oh, no. His trouble is mostly bronchial and I can give you some tablets to deal with that. He's not young, of course, but his general condition is pretty good for his age and his eyesight is still good.' She stroked the dog gently. 'You've been very well looked after, Georgie.'

After ushering her out Liz said cheerfully, 'No one in the waiting room at the moment. Shall we ask——' She stopped as the office door opened and Mark came out, to be joined in a few moments by Paul. Determined to keep apart from all friction, Joanna went quietly into the dispensary and busied herself among the drugs, but the two rooms were separated only by a wooden partition and Paul's deep voice could be heard quite clearly.

'I'm going to Kendall's Farm and then on to Broadlands Stud to take some blood tests. If you hear Clare sending anyone else out that way will you please remind her that that area is, roughly speaking, my territory and she must call me on the car radio?'

'Good grief!' Liz was plainly agitated. 'It's not up to me to pass on messages. That's Clare's job. I'm Joanna's nurse.' She paused. 'I'll have to ask her.'

It was no use hiding away, Joanna decided, and, turning her back on the drugs, she came out from behind the partition.

Paul grinned at her disarmingly. 'You probably think you've come into a madhouse—well, it's that at the moment, but it isn't going to last. This evening I'm going to see Mr Mayfield.'

'Why, may I ask, are you going to see Daddy?' Clare stood in the doorway gazing at them disdainfully and, as the two men turned to face her, Joanna saw that Paul's face was set and grim.

'To get things sorted out once and for all,' he said coldly. 'As I told you just now, you're making it impossible for us to see our particular cases through, and that's demoralising for a veterinary surgeon.'

Clare opened her mouth to speak, but Liz said quickly,

'Clare, I don't think you've met Joanna yet. Joanna—this is Clare Mayfield, a partner's daughter.'

'The senior partner,' Clare said coldly. 'Well—hello.' She turned away. 'I must get back to my work and so must you. I can hear barking in the waiting room.'

Joanna's face flushed angrily as Clare disappeared but, keeping careful control of herself, she gestured to Liz, who went to investigate.

Mark laughed. 'Poor Joanna! I expect you're beginning to think you've taken on the wrong job.'

'No, I don't think I have,' she said calmly. 'My job is to be in charge of the small animal side of this practice, and that's how it's going to be.'

He looked at her admiringly. 'Good for you! "If you can keep your head when all about you"—etc. All the same, you'll have to tread warily. That girl—' he nodded towards the office, 'can be very unpleasant if she takes a dislike to you.'

Joanna looked at him thoughtfully. 'Perhaps you're all dealing with her the wrong way. Surely she must have a good side to her nature.'

'Oh, yes—the social side,' Paul said scornfully. 'She can be absolutely charming when she's taken out. As we all know—' he added grimly, 'whenever a new vet—male—arrives here she's all over him, hinting that—well, as Mr Mayfield's daughter, an instant partnership awaits him if——' he stopped at the sight of Joanna's expression of disbelief. 'True, isn't it, Mark? You can vouch for that.'

Mark nodded, but Joanna turned away and went over to inspect the steriliser. Suddenly she looked back at them.

'I don't want to hear any more about Clare Mayfield. I think you're all ganged up against her. I'm sure she can't be as bad as you make out, so please don't involve me in all this feuding and fighting.'

The two men glanced at each other ruefully, then, as Liz brought a client into the room, they went quietly out to their cars.

For the next half hour Joanna was kept busy treating a variety of small animals, some with trivial problems quickly solved and others with serious troubles requiring careful diagnosis and painstaking explanations to their owners. Conscious at first that Clare had come out of the office and was listening, Joanna gradually forgot her presence. After all, she told herself, Mrs Holman had said it would not be for much longer, so any slight irritation must be endured patiently.

Surgery time was nearly over when the last patient was brought in, an old springer spaniel in a very distressed condition. Joanna studied the case history and when her examination was completed she shook her head slowly. 'I'm afraid there's only one thing to do,' she said slowly, and glanced up at the smartly dressed woman who stood frowning back at her. 'It's very sad for you but merciful for him.' She stopped and waited, stroking the dog's head compassionately.'

'Oh, no, I can't allow him to be put to sleep,' the woman's voice was hard and determined. 'I'm sure you could operate and put him right. Nearly right, anyhow,' she added. 'I don't mind how much it costs. I don't believe in giving in so easily.'

Joanna sighed. 'Mrs Ford, an operation will only put him through needless misery. He's already in pain and no injections or tablets are going to help for any length of time. He's fourteen years old—that's the equivalent of ninety-eight years in human terms.' She paused and looked appealingly at her client. 'I'm sure you love him too much to let him suffer unnecessarily.'

Mrs Ford shook her head angrily. 'I don't think it's unnecessary. Doctors perform wonderful operations on humans—why can't you do the same for a dog?'

Joanna's heart sank. How could she convince this woman that the cases were not the same? 'I doubt if any surgeon would operate on a ninety-eight-year-old patient in a case as hopeless as this,' she said quietly.

'Danny is not ninety-eight,' Mrs Ford said sharply, 'he's only fourteen. Ninety-eight—that's ridiculous!'

'No, really. It's perfectly true. Every year in a dog's life is equal to about seven of ours. If I operate I'm afraid it will be too much for him. Even if his heart—a very old heart—stands the anaesthetic, and I doubt it very much, he'll have to be so doped with painkillers that he'll probably die soon afterwards.'

'I'll take that risk,' Mrs Ford said firmly. 'When will you operate?'

Knowing she was beaten, Joanna said resignedly, 'As soon as possible, then. Tomorrow morning. Remember, nothing to eat or drink from this evening—that is if he's eating at all.'

'Well, no, he isn't,' Mrs Ford admitted. 'I have to force food into him, and it nearly always comes back.'

'Well, let him have his own way tonight. A little milk if he'll take that willingly.' Joanna paused, her heart wrung with pity for an animal under the care of such a ruthless owner. 'Please don't be surprised if he doesn't survive the operation.

Mrs Ford gazed at her thoughtfully for a long moment. Then, suddenly, she lifted the wasted sad old dog from the table and bending down, fixed on his lead. Then she looked up, her face flushed with anger.

'I don't trust you. You'll probably put him to sleep just to prove you're right. I'm going to take him to another vet.'

Dragging the poor dog, she marched out of the surgery, and Liz, shutting the door behind her, gasped indignantly,

'Of all the ghastly women! How could she be so cruel?'

Joanna said nothing. Her eyes were burning with unshed tears and she turned away to hide them. Suddenly she found herself facing Clare Mayfield, who stood in the open door of the office staring at her accusingly.

'You've lost us a client,' she said sharply. 'That's a fine start to your new job! You shouldn't have argued with her like that. She wanted you to operate—you should have agreed at once.'

'Good God!' Joanna's distress turned to burning anger. 'What right have you to criticise my professional judgement or the way in which I tried to make that callous woman spare her dog more suffering?'

'Well, you didn't succeed, did you?' Clare smiled spitefully. 'I wonder what my father will say when I tell him?'

Staring at her in incredulous disgust, Joanna was speechless, and Liz said quietly,

'Clare, you have no right to talk like that. You're not a veterinary surgeon and I'm sure your father would be horrified at your interference. You know very well that this is not a 'make work' practice. We're only concered with the welfare of animals.'

'Don't preach at me!' Clare's face suddenly paled. 'Just because you're a veterinary nurse you think you know everything!' Turning quickly, she went back into the office and slammed the door, leaving the two girls staring at each other in amazement.

CHAPTER TWO

LIZ spoke first. 'The trouble with that girl is that she has an enormous chip on her shoulder. Her father wanted her to become a vet, but she just wasn't up to it. Unfortunately, instead of taking up another kind of career she persuaded him to give her a job in the practice. The result is—' Liz shrugged, 'well, trouble all round.'

Joanna frowned. 'She can't go on interfering like this. Personally I hope she does tell her father about me losing a client, as she calls it. After all, he's a vet, so he's bound to see my point of view.' She paused. 'Paul is going to see him this evening, so that should bring matters to a head.'

'Let's hope so.' Liz didn't sound very optimistic. 'Anyhow, it's coffee time. I think I'll go and have mine with Mrs Holman. Will you come?'

Joanna hesitated. 'No, I don't think so,' she said at last. 'Another time, perhaps.'

'Well, there's a jar of instant coffee in the dispensary and milk in the fridge.' Liz went to the door. 'I'll be back in about half an hour. Ring through if you want me sooner than that.'

A few minutes later Joanna went into the office.

'Would you like to have coffee with me?' she asked calmly, and Clare, seated at the desk, turned and stared at her resentfully.

'I should have thought you would have preferred to go over to Ma Holman's and joined in the usual game of pulling me to pieces,' she said scornfully.

'Don't be silly,' Joanna said equably. 'I'm sure they've got something better to do. Would you like a biscuit? I found this tin beside the coffee.'

Pulling out a chair, she sat down and placed the mugs of coffee on the desk.

Clare's eyes narrowed. 'I suppose you think that by being friendly you can stop me telling my father about you losing a client,' she said spitefully.

'Nothing of the kind,' Joanna shook her head firmly. 'I don't mind you telling your father. I'll probably tell him myself when I see him. He's bound to understand, being a vet himself.'

'Ah, there you go! Getting at me—just like the others!' Clare banged her coffee mug on the desk, splashing some of the hot liquid over on to Joanna's surgery coat. 'Oh, damn! See what you've made me do!'.

Joanna wiped her coat with a tissue, then looked up with a frown. '"Getting at you?"—what on earth do you mean?'

The other girl flushed angrily. 'Just because I haven't any qualifications it doesn't mean I'm not just as good as you are. I may not be a vet, but my father owns this practice and you're all dependent on him.'

'Goodness,' Joanna burst out laughing, 'what an inferiority complex you've got!'

'Inferiority complex? Me?' Clare blinked in astonishment. 'You're crazy! I don't think I'm inferior to anybody.'

'Oh, but you do,' Joanna said softly. 'That's why you're so arrogant with everybody.' She paused. 'But you've got it all wrong. Just because you're not a vet it doesn't mean that you're less intelligent than the rest of us. Being a vet is a kind of vocation. But there are other careers, so why not go in for something that makes better use of your talents?'

Clare sipped her coffee, studying Joanna reflectively for a few minutes. Then she said coldly,

'I suppose you think I can't see through you. You want to get rid of me—that's obvious. Well, that's where you make a big mistake——' she stopped abruptly as the telephone rang.

Picking up the receiver, she listened, then said, 'A what? Cow with relapsed uterus? Hardacre Farm? Yes, I'll pass the message on to one of our vets. Who? Mr Copeland?

Well, I'm not sure. Anyhow someone will be with you soon.'

She rang off, then turning to Joanna she said coldly,

'I must put this through to——' she paused. 'Oh, well, anyone will do. I'll try Sandy.'

It was while Clare was speaking to Sandy on the car radio that Joanna remembered Paul's request. That and the fact that the caller had expressly asked for him seemed to indicate that the farm was in what Paul had said was his territory. She frowned. It was all so new to her and on this, her first day, she really didn't want any more trouble. She listened, then got up in alarm as she heard Clare say,

'Miles from where you are? Well, you'll just have to get there somehow. They said it was urgent.'

'Clare, don't you remember——' but it was too late. Clare slammed down the receiver and turned angrily.

'You still here?'

Joanna flushed but stood her ground. 'Yes. I want to make a note in the appointment book for an operation at eleven tomorrow morning. Liz said there were other things booked as well.'

Silently Clare handed the book over and, to Joanna's relief, there was nothing fixed for eleven o'clock. The only appointment was for the routine examination of a guide dog for the blind fixed for the evening surgery.

'I think——' Joanna shut the book and looked steadily at Clare, 'I think I'll keep this now. No doubt you have a separate book for large animals.'

'Yes, I have, but I'm in charge of all appointments. That's my job.' Clare stared at her defiantly.

'No, I think you're mistaken,' Joanna said firmly. 'I'm in charge of the small animal practice and must fix all appointments myself.'

For a few moments Clare looked as though she was going to argue, then suddenly she lowered her gaze. 'Oh, all right. I don't really care. It will save me work.'

'Exactly,' Joanna said smoothly. 'I'm sure it will be easier for both of us.'

Clare nodded, then unexpectedly she said, 'Thanks for the coffee anyway.'

Well, that at least was something, Joanna thought. It seemed that the best way to deal with such a difficult girl was to keep one's temper and try to understand her.

A few minutes later, back in the surgery, Joanna was studying the apppointments book when the telephone rang yet again and, Clare called from the office, 'You'd better deal with this. It's a query about a dog. Mrs Hillier wants some advice.'

Taking the receiver, Joanna listened for a while, then said, 'Well, I can't tell you without seeing the dog. If, as you say, he's got a bone stuck in his throat it must be dealt with at once.' Putting down the receiver, she smiled at Clare. 'It sounds more like swollen glands to me, but his mistress is convinced he's choking to death.'

'Oh, that's typical of Mrs Hillier. She's a friend of my mother and she's pretty stupid—Mrs Hillier, I mean. Always imagining her dog has got something terribly wrong. She worries the poor thing to death—he's nearly as neurotic as she is.'

'There are lots of people like that,' Joanna agreed. 'Mostly they live alone, so perhaps it's understandable.' She paused. 'Have you got a dog?'

Suddenly Clare's sullen face lit up. 'Yes. Rufus—he's a golden retriever—absolutely adorable! He needs plenty of exercise, of course, but I solve the problem by taking him with me when I go riding.' Suddenly, as though she was ashamed of her momentary friendliness, her smile faded and she turned away.

But it was enough for Joanna to see that underneath the disagreeable surface there was, after all, a very human girl. Now she felt more at ease and resolved to keep the atmosphere as friendly as possible.

When Liz returned and heard of Mrs Hillier's imminent arrival she laughed. 'There's probably nothing wrong with

the dog at all.' Then with a quick glance at the office door
she added softly, 'Perhaps I'd better warn you to be extra
tactful. Mrs Hillier is a friend of the Mayfields.'

Joanna smiled. 'I know. Clare told me when we had
coffee together.'

'Coffee together? She told you——' Eyes widening in
astonishment, Liz said, 'You're joking!'

'No,' Joanna said quietly. 'As you said, she's got a chip
on her shoulder, but underneath, she's not too bad.'

Liz shrugged. 'You could have fooled me. Still, if you say
so——' She stopped and went to the window. 'Here's Mrs
Hillier.'

All and more than Clare had foretold, Mrs Hillier was
anxious and over-protective of her corgi, excusing his
snappy, aggressive behaviour as being due to excessive pain.

'I'm sure there's a bone stuck in his throat,' she said
firmly. 'I gave him some pieces of chicken left over from
yesterday and it was immediately after this that the trouble
started. Usually he loves to crunch up the bones, but this
time after a few seconds he began gagging and was obviously
having difficulty in swallowing.'

'Chicken bones?' Joanna shook her head in dismay. 'You
should never give those to a dog. Still, let's see if by chance
one got lodged in his throat.'

Placed protestingly on the table, the corgi was difficult to
control, but under Liz's firm grasp and in spite of Mrs
Hillier's remonstrations, Joanna held the dog's tongue down
with the aid of a spatula. Examination of his throat
completed, she looked up, shaking her head.

'Nothing there. Now, let's see——' Feeling carefully
round the angle on both sides of the corgi's jaw, she nodded
her head. 'His glands are very swollen—that accounts for his
difficulty in swallowing. An injection of antibiotic and tablets
will soon put that right.' She glanced at Liz. 'Will you put
one c.c. in a syringe, please? I'll hold Dandy.'

But Liz relaxed her hold before Joanna was able to grip
him and, seizing his opportunity, the corgi snapped at her

hand.

'Oh dear! Oh, my goodness!' Mrs Hillier gave a sharp little scream. 'No, Dandy! Naughty boy!'

'It's all right,' Joanna laughed as she gazed at the teeth marks on the front of her hand, 'he hasn't drawn blood. No harm done.' Taking the syringe from Liz, she pushed the needle quickly into a muscle, then, as Dandy yelped protestingly, she rubbed the place firmly and handed him over to his mistress. 'The tablets to be given one three times a day. Make sure you get them down him.'

'But how?' Mrs Hillier frowned anxiously. 'I'll never be able to—oh, dear. What am I to do? He'll never let me——' She shook her head wildly. 'I'll just have to bring him in here three times a day.'

Joanna looked at her thoughtfully. No use showing her how to slip the tablets down. She would make a complete nonsense of it and would then blame Joanna because the dog did not make a quick recovery. Then, suddenly, her problem was solved by the unexpected appearance of Clare.

Hand outstretched, she came out of the office. 'Hello, Mrs Hillier. Hello, Dandy. I heard what you said about the tablets. Would you like me to drop in and give them to him? You live so near to us that it wouldn't be any trouble.'

Gratefully Mrs Hillier accepted, and Clare went outside with her, talking of family affairs, while Liz gaped open mouthed after them. At last, turning to Joanna, she said,

'What miracle did you work when you had coffee with her? Did you drop some magic potion in the cup?'

Joanna laughed. 'It's nothing to do with me. I think she's just naturally fond of dogs and wants to help.' She paused. 'There's the telephone. I'd better take it.'

Paul's voice was tense with anger. 'Why on earth did you let Clare send Sandy Wilson to that cow with the relapsed uterus? Mr Parker was most annoyed and said he didn't like getting a different vet when he asked expressly for me.' He paused, then added, 'Sorry, Joanna—I thought I was talking to Liz, but perhaps she wasn't there at the time. I'll just have to have it out with Clare. Is she there?'

'She's outside, talking to a client.' Joanna hesitated, then said slowly, 'actually I was there and heard enough to realise that Mr Parker was asking for you. I ought to have stopped her, but it was all rather quick and——'

'I know,' Paul said stiffly, 'you didn't want to get involved. Well, let me tell you, Joanna, that we all pull together in this practice—at least, we used to till that stupid girl began taking over. You should have made her contact me.'

Smarting at the rebuke, Joanna said angrily, 'I would remind you that this is my first day here, and I refuse to take the blame for Clare's carelessness. You must have it out with her, as you say. It's nothing to do with me.'

Quickly replacing the receiver, she drew a long breath, then, turning, she found herself facing Clare.

'My carelessness? How dare you criticise me? Who were you talking to?' Clare's eyes gleamed with fury.

'Paul,' Joanna said sharply. 'He was blaming me for allowing you to send Sandy Wilson out to that cow with the relapsed uterus.'

'So I'm careless, am I?' Clare's face whitened. 'You're as bad as the rest of them—making me out to be a fool! Paul's just making a mountain out of a molehill as usual.' She paused. 'Well, I'm going out to do some shopping and you can look after the beastly phone yourself.'

Turning on her heel, she marched out of the office, leaving Joanna shaking her head despairingly. How on earth was she going to get through the next few weeks with all this quarrelling going on? It took away all her pleasure in her work. Perhaps even it would destroy her concentration on her patients. Sitting down at the desk, she contemplated the future very pessimistically. At last she got up and went out to Liz, who had obviously overheard everything. To her surprise, Liz treated it all as a joke. 'Typical,' she said. 'Don't take it seriously. You'll get used to it.' She paused. 'Strictly between the two of us, there is a reason for the antagonism between Paul and Clare. They used to go around together at one time, then Paul just dropped her and she was furious. Now she's trying to take it out on him—a kind of revenge, I suppose.' She stopped, then added thoughtfully, 'Sometimes I think she's in love with him, but she's certainly not going the right way about it to get him back.'

'She ought to have more pride,' Joanna said scornfully. 'Anyhow, if that's the situation between them the sooner Clare goes back to her own office the better. They can do all their fighting over there.'

Liz laughed. 'I don't think Paul wants to do any fighting. All he's really interested in is his work. I think too that he only went out with Clare to find out what she was like. He's quite ruthless with girls—ditches them quite calmly when they begin to get serious.'

Joanna frowned. This kind of gossip was new to her and she didn't really care for it. Remembering her resolve not to get too involved with her colleagues at work, she made a noncommittal reply and set herself to studying some of the case-histories of former patients on the cards in the file.

At lunchtime Liz announced that she would be working in the hospital during the afternoon. 'No patients at the moment, thank goodness,' she said cheerfully, 'so after I've cleaned out I'll buzz off home. Chrissie will be in at two o'clock. I'll transfer the telephone up to your flat, if that's all right with you.' She paused. 'If, of course, you decide to go out for lunch I'll put it through to Mrs Holman. That's what we usually do. And the same thing when you have any outside calls to make.'

Joanna nodded. She had forgotten that she would have the chance sometimes to call on clients who were unable to get to the surgery. It would be a relief to get away from time to time. Her spirits lifted as she went up to her flat. All she needed was a sandwich and coffee and time to reflect on the happenings of the last few hours. It was all so very different from the quiet life she had led in Suffolk.

Ah, Suffolk! For a moment she wished she had never left that sleepy little town so near the sea that she used to love so dearly. Suddenly her eyes burnt with hot tears. The friendly North Sea on which she had spent so many glorious windswept hours with James until one day, with terrible suddenness, that same sea had become a malevolent enemy and killed all her dreams. Dreams that she soon discovered were wild fantasies founded on deception. To lose James had been bad enough, but to learn that she had been living in a fool's paradise—that was the ultimate disillusionment. She had been so near to giving way to the urgency of his lovemaking, believing his promise of a future life together, his vague hints of marriage—what a credulous fool she had been! Love, they said, was blind, and she was so much in love with him that his death by drowning had left her utterly desolate. She had so nearly been drowned herself—only rescued when almost unconscious—then, later, came the most terrible blow of all.

His hitherto unmentioned wife appeared on the scene. Even now Joanna could feel the searing pain that had pierced her through and through at the discovery of James' deceit. Her parents had been supportive, Mr Bridges had tried to help, but James' wife had been the object of sympathy in the village and she, Joanna, the butt of malicious gossip.

To get away from such a hateful atmosphere she had come to build up a new life among strangers—only to find that one of these strangers was strongly linked to Suffolk. Sipping her coffee reflectively, she faced up to the fact that when Paul Copeland next visited his family home he would probably learn of the tragedy that had occurred only a few months ago. His sister, he had told her, took her dog to Mr Bridges.

Joanna sighed, then tried to shrug off her uneasiness. What did it matter if Paul did find out? His opinion of her was of no importance. Gradually her depression lifted and, going over to the window, she stood for a few moments gazing down on to the yard. These new surroundings, this busy practice, would soon help her to forget.

Just as she was about to turn away, her attention was arrested by the sight of a car pulling up under the window. To her surprise she saw Paul Copeland get out, carrying a bundle wrapped in a blanket. Her professional instinct aroused, she hurried down the stairs and came face to face with him as he came through the surgery door.

'A casualty from Clayton Farm,' he said curtly, 'a whelping case that has gone on far too long. They're so busy harvesting out there that this poor little bitch has been forgotten. She was in her kennel outside and I saw her when I was leaving. Mrs Clayton thought it was just something that would right itself eventually. But it won't. She'll die if she doesn't have a Caesarian. Shall I do it or will you?'

Joanna hesitated. 'Well, she's your patient, but I'm the small animal vet.'

'All right, though I'd rather——' he paused, then added grimly, 'I haven't any option, I suppose.'

She glared at him indignantly. 'Do you doubt my ability?'

He hesitated, then shrugged. 'Not really. It's just that I——'

'I understand. You have no faith in anybody else. Well, I assure you——'

'Oh, for heaven's sake—' his mouth twitched angrily, 'Let's get on with it. This is urgent.' He paused. 'I'll anaesthesise her.'

Joanna bit her lip, then said calmly, 'Yes, you'll have to. Liz has gone and Chrissie hasn't arrived yet.'

She tried to hide her dismay at the thought of his supervising her operating technique and could feel her cheeks flushing at his quick, mocking glance. Almost immediately, however, professionalism took over and she pushed her resentment aside.

The black and white Border collie was desperately in need of help. Limp and exhausted, she was too tired even to whimper when given the anaesthetic and sank into unconsciousness almost immediately.

'Poor little bitch. Utterly helpless and no one caring a tuppenny damn,' Paul said quietly as though speaking to himself and, glancing up for a moment, Joanna saw such compassion in his eyes that she was taken by surprise. Cynical and hard as he had appeared to her at first, it seemed that when it came to animals, his feelings ran very deep. The realisation caused her nervousness to return. He was so much more experienced than she was, and this patient had gone almost to the limit of endurance. On the point of making the first incision, she hesitated for a split second, then, drawing a deep breath, she conquered what she knew to be quite unreasonable self-distrust.

Working quickly and confidently, she concentrated on her patient and soon lifted out the first puppy.

'Dead,' she said briefly, 'and so is this one.' Then as she drew out the third she added quickly, 'This one is OK and there's another—OK too, I think.' She paused. 'One more—yes, and that's alive as well.'

Paul was taking them from her as she handed them to him and he said quietly,

'I can leave her for a minute if you just watch the colour of the blood.'

'It's still nice and red. Well oxygenated.'

'Right.' Cleaning the puppies up quickly, he folded a blanket on top of them, then came back to the anaesthetic machine. As Joanna began suturing he said, 'I'll take her off now. She's doing fine, but I'll get two c.c.s of Millophyline to stimulate her heart, just in case.'

He stood watching silently as she sutured the muscle together and then began on the skin. Cutting off the last neat knot, she stood back with a sigh of relief.

The injection of Millophyline was slipped into the thigh muscle and Paul said quietly,

'Nice work.' He paused. 'I'll put her in the recovery cage. She should be all right now and when she's completely round her babies can be put in with her.'

'What a good job you brought her in,' Joanna said as they attended to the puppies. 'You certainly saved her life.'

'So did you,' he said, and suddenly he smiled—a warm, devastatingly attractive smile that caused her heart to give a little lurch. Quickly she pulled herself together and began cleaning up the operating table.

'No need for you to do that.' Paul looked amused. 'Chrissie will be in soon—that's her job. Didn't you have a veterinary nurse when you were with Mr Bridges?'

'She was only part-time and when she wasn't there I always did the necessary.' Joanna laughed. 'I'm not used to having such a lot of help!'

'Well, it's always good to be able to cope with everything. It makes one much more self-reliant.' He paused. 'Which do you prefer—a large practice or a small one?'

She hesitated. 'I hardly know yet. At the moment I find it rather confusing. So many people—all so different—I suppose I'll get it sorted out eventually.'

'Yes.' Gently he took the cloth from her. 'Stop it—remember you're the big white chief here. How about a coffee? I didn't have time for lunch.'

'Why, of course. You must be starving.' Impulsively she added, 'Come up to my flat. I can find you something—an omelette—bread and cheese——'

'That's an idea.' Paul stopped, then added half-mockingly, 'Do you think you should, though?'

'Should what?' Puzzled, Joanna turned to look at him enquiringly.

'Invite me up to your flat. It might cause a certain amount of talk around here, you know.' He paused, then added a little drily, 'Of course, if you don't mind people whispering behind your back——'

'Oh, God!' To his amazement she went deathly pale. 'I've had enough——' She stopped, then seeing his astonishment she took a grip on herself. 'I see what you mean. Look, I'll go up and get you a sandwich.'

'No, don't bother,' he shook his head, 'I'll nip across to

Ma Holman. She loves ministering to hungry vets, but I would like a coffee first.'

His eyes were still puzzled as he watched her fill the kettle and suddenly he asked,

'What on earth was the meaning of that little outburst?'

Angry at having betrayed herself, Joanna said coldly, 'Nothing really. Just that I wouldn't like people to get the wrong impression of me. Do you take sugar?'

'No, thanks, and I'll have it black, please.'

She could feel his eyes on her as she handed him the mug of coffee but resolutely refused to meet his gaze.

'I seem to have touched on a sore point,' he said quietly, 'so I'd better change the subject. You told me your parents live in Suffolk. Were you born there?'

'No. They only moved there a couple of years ago when my father retired. They used to spend holidays there and the air suits them.'

'It is good, isn't it?' he said enthusiastically, 'and the sea—I love the North Sea. Grey and menacing in winter and that beautiful green colour in summer. One day fairly soon I hope I'll set up there on my own. Somewhere about ten miles from the coast, and that way I'll have the country and still be near the coast. Do you like sailing?'

'No—not——' her hands in her overall pockets clenched tightly, but she managed to keep her voice under control. 'I don't much care for the sea.'

'Really? Good lord, I thought everyone did—but I suppose I'm biased.'

Joanna could stand it no longer. Something snapped inside her and her mouth quivered as she said fiercely,

'Oh, for heaven's sake stop talking about Suffolk and the sea! I've come here to get away from——' she stopped aghast and her eyes dropped before his astonished gaze. 'I'm sorry,' she said inadequately as his brows drew together in any angry frown, 'I can't explain——'

'No need to,' his voice was very cold, 'you've made it perfectly clear that you find my conversation excessively boring. Thank you for the coffee.'

Joanna stood gazing at the closed door. Why, oh, why had she been so stupid? To lose her self-control so easily and, what was perhaps worse, to have her outburst so wrongly interpreted. No man liked being thought a bore. She would have to put that right. But how on earth could she do that without giving him the real reason for not wanting to talk about Suffolk? Slowly she shook her head. She could never tell Paul, comparative stranger that he was, all that she had undergone, and there was no likelihood that he would believe her. Blinking back hot tears of regret, she faced the fact that it was best to leave things as they were. He would dislike her from now on—that was inevitable—but there was no alternative.

CHAPTER THREE

JOANNA'S troubled thoughts were interrupted by the arrival of Chrissie. Tall, slim, silky dark hair cut close to her head, she greeted Joanna with a smile that lit up her rather pale face. As soon as she was told of the Caesarian operation she looked down at the operating table.

'You've cleaned up,' she said, 'thank you very much, but no need to do it in future. That's my job,' she laughed, 'general factotum—otherwise dogsbody—that's me. Talking of dogs—how's the patient?'

They went over to look at the bitch in the recovery cage and Joanna said, 'I don't think there'll be any complications—she's beginning to come round already.'

'Sweet little puppies—' Chrissie looked them over, 'I'll get them on to their mother as soon as she's ready for them.' She stopped as the telephone rang, then, as Clare's voice was heard, Chrissie jerked her head towards the office. 'How are you getting on with her?'

Joanna hesitated for a moment, then shrugged lightly. 'Not too badly—reasonably well, I suppose.'

Chrissie smiled sceptically. 'Perhaps you'll be able to manage her—if so, you'll be the first one. Apart from Paul, that is.' She paused, then added slowly, 'This is a nice practice with only one fly in the ointment, and that's Clare Mayfield.'

'Talking about me as usual?' The bitter interruption made them jump as Clare suddenly appeared in the open doorway. 'Honestly, I wonder why I stand it!'

'Well, why do you?' Chrissie's voice was sharp. 'If you're not happy here why not go somewhere else? Find a different kind of job.'

Joanna's heart sank at the prospect of another row. Chrissie's open antagonism did not bode well for the future.

'Look, this is my domain,' she said firmly. 'No more unpleasant remarks, please.'

Clare turned back into the office, shutting the door behind her.

'Not suprising that Jean Russell left, is it?' Chrissie said reflectively. 'She was never able to assert her authority with anyone. Perhaps things will improve now you're here. They couldn't really get any worse. Sandy Wilson is leaving soon—not that he's any great loss—but I've been terrified that Mark might——' She stopped, then the colour rose in her cheeks as she met Joanna's curious glance. Half laughingly, she added ruefully, 'Yes, that's how it is with me, but I haven't a hope, I know.' She stopped, then said quickly, 'I'm talking too much. I'd better get on with my work. By the way, have you any outside calls this afternoon?'

'No, thank goodness. I don't know my way round here very well though I did do a bit of exploring over the weekend. I think I'll go up to my flat for a while—there are one or two things I'd like to do——' Joanna stopped as someone passed the window, 'I spoke too soon.'

'It's all right. It's only Paul,' Chrissie said. 'Come to see the patient, I expect.'

He greeted Joanna coldly and gave Chrissie a friendly smile. 'Just come to make sure mother and babies are OK so that I can tell Mrs Clayton.'

'Coming round beautifully,' Chrissie said cheerfully. 'Do you want her to stay here the night?'

'Well, yes, she should.' Paul glanced at Joanna. 'However, that's for you to decide.'

She nodded. 'Yes, she should stay. Will you ring the farm?'

He made the call and was on the point of leaving when suddenly Clare appeared in the doorway.

'Just a moment, Paul—I'd like to speak to you. Will you come in here, please—it's rather private.'

'Oh, for heaven's sake—I'm in a hurry. It can't be all that private. What do you want?' He held the door handle. 'Say it now.'

'All right, though I think you might——' She saw he had no intention of giving in and said quickly, 'You said you'd be going up to see my father this evening. Well, he's down in Gloucestershire and spending the night there. So your complaint about me will have to wait. Anyway—' she paused, 'I—I'd be glad if you would forget it. It won't occur again.'

Paul stared at her, his dark brows raised in astonishment. Then he shrugged indifferently. 'OK, I'll leave it at that.'

Clare's eyes lit up. 'Hold on a minute. I've something else to ask you.' She glanced meaningly at Joanna, then at Liz, and the two girls, taking the broad hint, withdrew tactfully into the dispensary.

Turning on a tap, Joanna ran water over the coffee cups in the sink, but Chrissie made no secret of the fact that she was listening intently to the low-voiced conversation on the other side of the wooden partition.

Determined to keep aloof from all friction, Joanna paid no attention to the dismay on Chrissie's face when, as the outside door closed and the office door slammed, she gasped,

'Did you hear that?'

'No, and I don't want to know,' Joanna said sharply, then at the sight of Chrissie's stricken expression she relented. 'Oh, all right, tell me, if it will make you feel better.'

Chrissie blinked hard, obviously near to tears. 'Clare said she'd been given two tickets for the local theatre tomorrow evening and asked if Paul would go with her.'

'Well,' Joanna looked puzzled, 'why does that upset you? I thought it was Mark who——'

'Ah, yes, but when Paul refused—said he had another engagement—he suggested she should ask Mark as he's very fond of the theatre.'

'Does Paul know how you feel about Mark?'

Chrissie nodded miserably. 'I'm sure he does. Everyone here knows except Mark.' Her voice was bitter, and Joanna felt a surge of anger towards Paul.

'Well, that was unkind. But you may be wrong—he may not know, after all.'

Chrissie shook her head. 'I'm sure he does. He made a kind of sarcastic remark about it when we were having tea with Mrs Holman some time ago.' She shrugged listlessly. 'The trouble is he's so cynical about other people's love affairs that he simply doesn't care. He's only concerned about avoiding any entanglements himself.'

'Have you ever been out with Mark?'

'Twice.' Chrissie gave a wry smile. 'He seemed to like me, but he's never asked me out again, so I must have slipped up somewhere.'

'Not necessarily,' Joanna said sharply. 'Anyhow, why don't you copy Clare and ask him to take you to something special? I'll bet she bought those theatre tickets herself.'

'Perhaps she did, but I could never——'

'Oh, don't be so old-fashioned! At least he'll learn that you're interested in him.'

Chrissie stared for a moment, then she sighed. 'I don't think I could.'

'Don't be silly. If he refuses—well, you're no worse off, and if he accepts then—' Joanna laughed, 'I don't see why you should be coy about asking him. The Victorian age is long past.'

'Would you do that if you wanted to go out with someone? Paul, for instance.'

'Goodness, what an idea!' Joanna made a face. 'Certainly not Paul. But your case is different. You've already been out with Mark twice, so why shouldn't you ask him in return? Anyhow, that's my advice. You must do what you think best.' She paused as a car pulled up outside. 'That sounds like a client.'

Chrissie glanced out of the window. 'It's Mark—oh, goodness! Now Clare will ask him.'

'I've lost my stethoscope.' Mark came in looking irritable. 'Is there a spare one around, Chrissie?'

'I'll see.' She darted off to the store room and Mark said, 'Can't think where I've left it. Still, I suppose it will turn up somewhere—ah, thank you, Chrissie. You've saved my life. I need it to vet a horse.' He turned to Joanna. 'How are you getting on here? Do you think you'll like this part of the country? Ma Holman tells me you've come from the wilds of East Anglia. I've never been there, but I know Sussex very well.' He paused, gazing at her reflectively. 'Would you like to come out with me one of these days and let me show you some of my favourite places?'

Joanna was just going to say yes when she caught a quick glimpse of Chrissie's stricken face. 'Some time, perhaps,' she said vaguely and, pretending not to see his downcast look, she went quickly up to her flat.

An hour later Chrissie rang through.

'A rabbit with an abscess on its face, and the owner is bringing in a dog as well. Booster injection. Oh, and, by the way, Mrs Holman asks if you'd like to drop in for tea. She said don't bother to ring. If you don't turn up she'll know you're busy.'

Back in the surgery Joanna looked searchingly at Chrissie.

'Well, I left you alone with Mark. Did you ask him?' She glanced cautiously towards the office door. 'Or did Clare grab him first?'

'She never came out, and Mark went off in a hurry. But I will take your advice. There's a film showing locally—it's about Africa and there's a lot of wild life in it. Should be interesting for him. I'm just hoping Clare

won't ask him to the theatre after all.' She went towards
the waiting room. 'I think the rabbit and dog have
arrived.'

It was a nasty abscess and the frightened rabbit was
difficult to control. Twice it attempted to jump off the
table, but at last Chrissie held it firmly enough for Joanna
to freeze the swollen area.

'What a revolting sight!' Chrissie shuddered. 'I ought
to be hardened by now, but that's definitely horrible.'

Joanna laughed as she finished draining the abscess and
then injected antibiotic into the cavity. The owner, a large
lady accompanied by a teenage boy holding a dog on its
lead, sighed with relief. 'Thank goodness! I was afraid it
might have been a malignant growth.' She turned to her
son. 'Why, Freddie, your face is practically green! You
shouldn't have come in to watch.'

'Perhaps not,' he gulped, then gave a selfconscious
grin. 'I was thinking of becoming a vet, but I'm not so
sure now.'

Joanna smiled. 'Well, you've got plenty of time to
make up your mind. It's certainly not a job for the
squeamish, but it's very worthwhile.' She peeled off her
protective gloves. 'Now let's give your dog his booster.'

As soon as they had gone Joanna said, 'Well, I'll nip
over to Mrs Holman. Let me know if—' She stopped as he
office door opened and Clare appeared.

'I'm just off to the shops,' she said. 'I'll be about an
hour.'

Chrissie smiled wryly as the door closed. 'I like that!
She seems to think she can come and go as she pleases!'

'Well, it's your gain, isn't it?' Joanna said calmly.
'Now if Mark comes in again you can do your stuff.'

'Oh, I don't——' Chrissie hesitated, then added
slowly, 'I think he's more interested in you. He's never
asked me to go on his rounds with him.'

'Oh, for goodness' sake!' Joanna said impatiently.
'Don't be so feeble. In any case, he'll get nowhere with

me. I'm determined not to get involved with anyone in this practice. I don't believe in mixing personal relations with work, so you need have no worries on that score.'

Walking across to the Holmans' house, Joanna reflected on her last remark. It was a good thing to make her position clear to everyone. There was enough trouble in the practice as it was. She smiled as she entered Mrs Holman's kitchen, but that smile faded at the sight of Paul Copeland sitting at the table.

He greeted her coolly and sat silently watching Mrs Holman as she put some small cakes on the table.

'Home baked,' she said proudly, then laughed ruefully. 'Not terribly professional, but the ingredients are good.'

'They're lovely,' Joanna nibbled appreciatively. 'It's nice of you to ask me to tea.'

'You mustn't wait to be asked in future. Just drop in—it's open house. I like it that way and it keeps me up to date with all the goings on in the practice.' Mrs Holman laughed and corrected herself hastily, 'What I mean is that I hear about interesting cases. For instance, Paul has been telling me about a donkey he's been seeing. Poor thing—it was in a terrible state. He was called in by the RSPCA. Tell Joanna about it, Paul.'

He looked up frowningly. 'Well, I don't want to bore you,' he paused, the silvery eyes glinting a little as he saw her colour rise. 'Would you be interested? Small animals are more in your line, aren't they?'

'Don't be silly,' Joanna returned his gaze scornfully, 'I love all animals, and donkeys appeal to me very much. I used to have one when I was a small girl. I loved her dearly.'

'Did you? Well, this donkey hasn't had any affection at all—a poor neglected creature in a terrible state. Emanciated—bones nearly piercing its skin, its feet so overgrown it could hardly walk—utterly sad and lonely. Donkeys need companionship, as you must know, and this one has been left tied up in an open shed. Apparently roaming tinkers had left it there when they moved on.'

'Couldn't someone have reported it before it got into that state?' Mrs Holman asked. 'Surely the locals——'

'It was in an isolated part at the bottom of the Old Common woods. Some children discovered it.' Paul paused, then added, 'The RSPCA inspector thought it ought to be put to sleep, but I'd like to give it a chance. It's only about four years old. I've got the local farrier to see its feet—a difficult job, I know, but he's going to do his best. He's a decent chap and he's taken it over to his place to begin the work. By the way,' Paul turned to Mrs Holman, 'I'm paying for this treatment myself because I'd like to be responsible for the animal.'

'What do you plan to do with it when the farrier considers it's fit to move?'

'Well, I'm not sure.' Paul looked thoughtfully. 'Perhaps get her into a donkey sanctuary or, if she recovers enough, let her go as a pet to a country family.'

'A donkey sanctuary is a good idea,' Joanna said, 'and, later on—if she's fit enough—why not give her to a home for physically and mentally disabled children? She would make a marvellous pet, helping them in many ways either for riding or pulling a little cart with one or two children as passengers.

Paul looked at her curiously. 'You seem to know a lot about it. Have you actually seen one kept in a home like that?'

'There was one about ten miles from Mr Bridges' practice. He looked after their animals and sometimes I went with him. They had a donkey and the children adored it.'

'It's a very good idea,' Paul smiled, and the coldness left his eyes as he spoke to her. 'I'll make enquiries and see if there's a similar place in this area, always provided we can offer them a reliable and safe animal. But first of all I want to get her well. There's a donkey sanctuary about twenty miles from here where I think she would be properly tended. How about coming with me to see if it's suitable and, if so, whether they'd take her in?'

Joanna hesitated, wanting to accept yet unable to quell the doubt in her mind, but Mrs Holman was enthusiastic.

'You'd like that, Joanna, and you'd see a bit of this part of the world at the same time. You must try and work it so that your days off coincide.'

Then suddenly, just as she was about to say yes to his invitation, Joanna saw that Paul had put his own interpretation on her silence. With a hint of sarcasm in his voice he said,

'Perhaps it's not such a good idea after all. It would be too much of a busman's holiday for you. I expect you'd rather get away from the veterinary side of life when you have a day off.'

It was plain that he regretted having asked her so impulsively, and, furious at having been snubbed in front of Mrs Holman, Joanna quickly covered her embarrassment.

'There's something in what you say,' she said coolly. 'In any case, you won't need my opinion as to whether the sanctuary would be suitable.'

'True,' he nodded indifferently, then, turning to Mrs Holman who was gazing at them both in obvious astonishment, he added, 'thank you for the tea. Now I must be off.'

As the door closed behind him Mrs Holman frowned. 'What on earth went wrong there? Did I say something tactless?'

'No, of course not.' Joanna forced a bright smile. 'But I don't particularly want to spend a precious day off in his company.'

Mrs Holman's eyes widened in surprise. 'Don't you like him, then?'

Joanna shrugged. 'I don't really know him. But he's right when he says I'd rather get away from my work when I have time off.'

'You're like my husband,' Mrs Holman said thoughtfully. 'He always maintains that one should have interests outside the surgery. Perhaps—' she hesitated, then said carefully, 'is there someone——?' She stopped. 'No, I shouldn't ask that—I'm just being nosy. Will you have some more tea?'

Joanna laughed. 'No more, thank you, and you needn't apologise like that. As a matter of fact there isn't anyone at the moment. I'm quite fancy free and prefer to stay that way.'

'Ah, well,' her hostess smiled, 'I expect you're wise. But I must admit I'm surprised that Paul hasn't made a better impression on you. I rather thought——'

'That's because I'm not the susceptible type,' Joanna said lightly, and turned the conversation on to other things. But underneath her nonchalant manner there was deep anger at what she decided was Paul Copeland's arrogance. Admittedly, she herself had snubbed him when he was being so enthusiastic about Suffolk, but he needn't have taken his revenge in front of Mrs Holman. It was galling too, because the case of the neglected donkey really did interest her and she would, she acknowledged ruefully to herself, have loved to visit the donkey sanctuary.

Suddenly she realised that Mrs Holman was still talking about Paul. 'It's his weekend off. He told me he's going to visit his parents in Suffolk. That's where you come from, isn't it?'

'Yes.' Suddenly tense, Joanna glanced quickly at her watch. 'Goodness, I must fly! I've got several things to do before evening surgery.'

Walking back, she tried to calm her agitation. Why should she worry so much about Paul finding out about her past? There was nothing in it for which she should be ashamed and if the local gossip came to his ears, what did it matter? She and Paul would never be friends, so his opinion of her was valueless. Comforted by such sensible reasoning, Joanna relaxed and began to attend to the patients who were already gathering in the waiting room.

Mrs Turner, a middle-aged lady, arrived promptly for her appointment and was led in by a Labrador wearing the harness of a guide dog for the blind.

Joanna waited until the dog was free before stroking and praising her up, knowing that a guide dog should never be petted while on duty.

'That's right,' Mrs Turner said approvingly. 'I make a great fuss of her when she's at home, but she must never be distracted when she's wearing her harness.'

She sat on the chair that Chrissie held for her and waited in silence while Joanna did the routine examination. It was extensive, as everything had to be checked to make sure that the dog was perfectly fit. Susie's ears, her eyes, feet, her glands were done first, then Joanna sounded her heart, scaled her teeth and examined her skin. Finally, after asking Mrs Turner a few questions, she filled all the information into the booklet provided by the Guide Dogs' Association and handed it back.

'She's in great form. I've entered it all into her dossier, signed it, and now you can send the counterfoil back.'

Mrs Turner nodded gratefully. 'Susie is my lifeline. I count her as my greatest blessing.'

When she had gone Chrissie said thoughtfully, 'It brings a lump to my throat every time I see Mrs Turner. She's a widow living with her sister. She never grumbles and, in spite of her blindness, she lives a very full life. She takes long train journeys all over the country, giving lectures and visiting homes for the blind. When you see someone like that it puts all one's petty problems in perspective, doesn't it?'

Chrissie's words stayed in Joanna's mind when, after surgery was over, she returned to her flat. Her problems were indeed small by comparison. The past still haunted

her, but this new life would soon lay that ghost. As for the
tension in the practice—well, she must see to it that she
did not get too involved. Without being unfriendly she
would keep her personal life as private as possible.

Next morning, however, another problem presented
itself in the form of Sandy Wilson. Joanna had gone down
to the surgery half an hour early when suddenly the door
opened and a rather stockily built young man with a mop
of red hair came in.

'Sandy Wilson——' he held out his hand. 'I need to
look up something in the farming file.' He stood holding
her hand tightly until at last she pulled it firmly away. But
instead of going over to the filing cabinet he remained
staring at her. At last he said, 'Yes, they were right.
You're a stunner.'

She returned his searching look unsmilingly. 'How do
you do,' she said coolly. 'You're the vet who is leaving to
go into the Min of Ag, I believe.'

'That's right,' he paused and surveyed her calmly from
head to foot, 'though now I'm not so sure that I wouldn't
rather stay here.'

'What a stupid thing to say,' Joanna said scornfully,
and made to pass him on her way to the dispensary. But,
to her dismay, his arm slid round her waist and tightened
as she tried to get away.

'Come on, be friendly. Hell, who's that?' He turned
sharply as the outer door opened.

'Sorry to interrupt.' Paul Copeland stood on the
threshold for a moment, then, his face expressionless,
went past them to the telephone.

Sandy smiled unpleasantly. 'Tactful chap, our Paul,'
he said softly, then gave a sudden yelp of pain as Joanna
trod purposefully on his foot. Releasing her quickly, he
stood back and glared at her. 'That was a bit
unnecessary,' he said angrily. 'No need to cripple me.
That hurt!'

'It was meant to,' Joanna snapped. 'I'd be glad if you

would keep your distance. I don't like men who make
nuisances of themselves.'

He shrugged. 'The iceberg type, I see. Well, all the more
exciting.'

She moved away but he followed her closely until,
exasperated, she turned and faced him. 'For goodness' sake!
Stop pestering me!' then, glancing quickly in Paul's
direction, she saw that with one ear to the telephone, he was
watching them with an amused expression on his face that
was nearly as annoying as Sandy's behaviour. Angrily, she
made for the door leading up to her flat, but Sandy took a
quick step forward and blocked the way.

'No need to take offence,' he said smoothly, 'I was only
fooling. In any case Paul is here to protect you.'

There was a click as Paul replaced the receiver. 'I don't
think my protection is called for,' he smiled sardonically.
'That was a nice piece of footwork, Joanna.'

Sandy grinned shamefacedly. 'Never had my advances
spurned so forcibly.'

'Serve you right,' Paul said unfeelingly. 'Well, I have to
go. Are you sure you can cope with your amorous admirer
on your own, Joanna?'

'Of course I can,' Joanna said curtly, and Sandy laughed
derisively.

'Not very gallant, are you, Paul? Still, I suppose you've
got every reason to be a bit hard where women are
concerned.'

To Joanna's surprise, Paul's face turned noticeably pale
but he said nothing until he reached the door. Then very
softly he said, 'Lay off, Sandy, or you'll be sorry.'

'Hm!' Sandy stood looking after him. 'Touched on a raw
spot there, didn't I? Ah, well——' Ignoring Joanna, he went
into the office and began searching through the files.

It was during a break in morning surgery when Paul's
name came up in conversation that Joanna recalled the
curious little incident. Half jokingly she told Liz of Sandy's
behaviour.

'Oh, that's typical,' Liz laughed. 'Sandy thinks he's God's gift to women. We're all rather glad he's leaving at the end of this month. Even Clare doesn't like him, and that's saying something, because she's done her best to hook every vet we've ever had.'

'Ssh!' Joanna glanced warningly at the office door behind which Clare was ensconced. She had actually greeted them civilly this morning and Joanna had no wish to stir up unnecessary trouble.

Liz shrugged indifferently. 'Did you say Paul came in and stopped Sandy's little game?'

'Well—not exactly. He seemed rather amused.'

'Amused? Yes, he would be, of course.'

'Why ''of course''? And why did he look so odd when Sandy said something about him being hard where women are concerned?'

'Ah, that's quite a story.' Liz went towards the waiting room. 'There's someone here. I'll tell you later.'

The patients that morning were mostly routine cases and, apart from one or two highly nervous animals, surgery passed off smoothly.

Then Joanna said, 'I'm having coffee here. I don't like taking too much advantage of Mrs Holman's kindness. Will you ask Clare if she would like to join us?'

Liz made a face. 'Do you think that's a good idea? Let sleeping dogs lie is my motto.'

Joanna shook her head in mock disapproval, then, seeing Liz's reluctance to ask Clare, she herself went towards the office. Opening the door, she stopped abruptly on the threshold. Clare was sitting at the desk, her head in her hands, the picture of desolation. For a moment Joanna hesitated, then, quietly shutting the door behind her, she went up and put her arm round the girl's shoulder.

'Clare, what's wrong? Aren't you well?'

'Leave me alone.' Clare's shoulder stiffened and Joanna took her arm away.

'Do tell me,' she said compassionately, 'perhaps I can

help.'

'No one can help,' Clare lifted a ravaged face. 'I'm just utterly fed up, that's all. Paul, Mark—you all hate the sight of me.'

'Well, I don't,' Joanna said stoutly. 'I think you've got a very nice side to your character. You love animals and that's always a good thing in my eyes. I don't like to see you so upset—come and have a coffee with us.'

'You'll only laugh at me behind my back. Everybody does.'

'Nothing of the kind.' Joanna paused. 'Look, I'll bring my coffee in here with you and we'll have it on our own and perhaps we can sort things out.'

'I don't think—oh, all right. Perhaps you can help me after all. You're so new here—you probably see things from a different point of view.'

Liz, told that Clare wanted to talk over something, said meaningly, 'I suppose she wants you to be her friend. Be careful, Joanna. She tried that on Chrissie once and then let her down. Betrayed all her confidences.'

Sipping her coffee in silence, Clare seemed reluctant to begin, and Joanna, wary of making a false step, began talking about Mrs Turner and her guide dog.

'I know her well.' Clare's interest was aroused at last. 'I've done a bit of work for the Guide Dogs' Association. That kind of thing interests me.' She stopped then said suddenly, 'Do you think I ought to get another job? I'm not terribly good at this one—it bores me to death anyway—and I'm made to feel an interloper by everyone?'

'An interloper? Oh, surely not! How could you be? You're part of the practice, like—well, Mrs Holman. Everyone likes her. You could take a leaf out of her book, you know.'

'Don't be stupid,' Clare said resentfully. 'Ma Holman is a kind of mother figure, whereas I'm either looked upon as a spy in the camp or a rival to the girls.'

A rival?' Joanna looked puzzled for a moment, then

remembered Chrissie, and Clare, watching her carefully, saw the change in her expression.

'Yes, I know for a start that Chrissie likes Mark and thinks I'm out to get him.'

'Are you?'

'Of course not. He's dull and serious. I can't be bothered with him, and in any case he doesn't like me. As for Sandy—loathsome type! That leaves Paul——' She stopped suddenly and bit her lip. 'Well, that's another matter altogether.'

Suddenly overwhelmed by curiosity, Joanna managed to keep her face impassive. 'Yes,' she said carefully, 'he's a different proposition. He's far too cynical about everyone.'

Clare stared at her. 'You seem to have summed him up very quickly. Yes, he's cynical, and it's my fault. I played a nasty trick on him some time ago. He never knew it was a lie, but it's left me with an awful feeling of guilt. I ought to own up, I suppose. But it's too late now to put matters right.'

'You're talking in riddles.' Joanna was shocked at the note of despair in Clare's voice. 'Tell me more and I'll see if I can advise you.'

Clare hesitated, then said slowly, 'I don't want to go into details, but I broke up his love affair with a friend of mine. It changed Paul completely. Changed me too.'

Seeing that Clare was on the verge of tears, Joanna said gently, 'I expect you're blaming yourself too much. It might have just come to a natural end.'

'No,' Clare said vehemently, 'I was responsible. He adored her—wanted to marry her.' She paused. 'Now she's married someone else.'

'She couldn't have been all that serious about Paul then, could she?' Joanna said drily.

'No, perhaps not. But Paul was—deadly serious. It hit him hard.'

There was silence in the room for a few minutes. Then Joanna looked up from her coffee. 'Paul doesn't seem to me to be a man with a broken heart. In any case, hearts don't break that easily, as I well know.' She stopped as she saw Clare glance at her curiously, then added quickly, 'What's past is past. If Paul is cynical now about women what does it matter? Are you—' she hesitated, 'are you in love with him?'

'Oh no,' Clare shook her head. 'I thought I was once and that's why—well, I was jealous. It was a rotten thing to do and I don't think I'll ever feel right until I tell him. That's why I stay on here, hoping for an opportunity to own up.'

Joanna frowned. 'It seems to me that you would only make matters worse. My advise is to try and forget it. It might be better if you did get another job—something well away from here—but that's up to you. Meantime why not try to be more friendly towards the rest of us?'

Clare sat for a moment in silence. 'All right,' she said at last. 'Just so long as you don't tell anyone what I've said.'

When Joanna returned to the consulting room Liz looked at her questioningly, but the arrival of an emergency put an end to her curiosity.

'Hit by a lorry!' The agitated owner held out a small terrier and placed it on the table. 'The driver never stopped. I don't think he even noticed. 'Timmy wasn't actually run over, but one of those great wheels sent him flying into the gutter. Now he doesn't seem able to move—just whimpers when I touch him.'

A careful examination and then Joanna looked up. 'No bones broken,' she announced. 'I think it's mostly bad bruising and shock. I'll give him an injection and keep him in for observation in case of any internal bleeding. Come back this evening and hopefully he'll be all right.'

Liz was just settling the terrier into a warm recovery cage when Clare came out of the office.

'A call from Paul,' she said. 'He wants to know if the stable in the yard is empty—he's bringing a donkey in.' She turned to Joanna. 'Apparently you know all about the case. He says the farrier can't keep it after all.'

'Yes, I heard about it yesterday, but I don't know about the stable—I didn't even know there was one here.' Joanna glanced at Liz. 'Is it empty?'

She nodded cheerfully. 'All clean and ready. It's at the far end of the yard.' She laughed. 'A donkey—that'll make a nice change! Tell us about it, Joanna.'

As she unfolded the story Joanna noticed with relief that the atmosphere between the two girls was much more pleasant. Full of sympathy for the donkey's plight, Clare dropped her arrogant manner and when at last she returned to the office Liz opened her eyes wide and looked at Joanna meaningly.

'She's a different girl. What miracle have you worked?'

'Nothing to do with me,' Joanna laughed. 'She's a bit mixed up, that's all. Animals in trouble seem to bring out the best in her.'

Liz nodded. 'She was all right when she first started working here, but soon afterwards she changed. It was to do with——'

'Not now,' Joanna glanced at the office door, and Liz said,

'OK. Later—when we're alone.'

Remembering her promise to Clare, Joanna knew she must be careful. Probably Liz knew no more than she herself had been told by Clare, but she must not let that be discovered. It might be better to pretend she was not interested and not give Liz the opportunity to gossip.

But when Clare went to lunch Liz announced that she was going to wait for the arrival of the donkey and, standing by the window watching the entrance to the yard, she said,

'The mysterious affair of Paul, Clare and Clare's friend—would you like to hear it now?'

Joanna frowned. 'Oh, I don't know. It seems a bit mean to talk about people behind their backs. I expect it was all very trivial.'

Liz looked surprised. 'I thought you were interested. And it certainly wasn't trivial. I'll tell you anyway—it will pass the time. There was this girl, Fiona—lovely creature—Clare's friend. She came to one of our practice parties—Clare invited her. Up till then Clare had been going around with Paul, but as soon as he saw Fiona it was plain to us all that Clare's time was up. She was furious, of course, but there was nothing she could do as Paul was obviously only interested in Fiona. They went around together for about three months, then suddenly, wham! it was off. Paul was shattered and withdrew completely into himself and we never saw Fiona again. Naturally, as she was Clare's friend or had been once, we—Chrissie and I—asked Claire if she knew what had happened. She said she hadn't a clue, that Fiona didn't confide in her, but she looked jolly guilty and we were convinced she knew but wasn't telling. The last we heard was that Fiona had married a doctor and had gone to live in Shropshire or somewhere. I don't think Paul has ever got over it, and that's why he looked so strange when Sandy taunted him as you told me.' She stopped suddenly. 'Look, here comes the horsebox. Let's go out and make friends with the donkey.'

Watching the sad little creature being gently led into the stable, the two girls gasped in horror. Terribly emaciated, its bones sticking out under the ragged coat, it moved slowly and agonisingly on its overgrown feet, grotesque in their deformity. It drew tears to Joanna's eyes and Liz said in a shaken voice, 'They'll never get her right. I've never seen such a bad case.'

'Nor have I,' Joanna said sorrowfully, then turned as Paul came up to them.

'I know what you're thinking and you may well be right. The farrier says it will be a long job and the damage done might be permanent, but he's promised to do his best. It will be difficult for her to re-establish her new balance because the tendons have been stretched so much. Horton, the farrier, will come here to work on her and I just hope that with careful nursing we'll get her fit enough to go to a donkey sanctuary.' He turned to Liz. 'I'm going to set up rules for feeding that you and Chrissie must stick to rigidly. The temptation to overfeed in view of her obvious malnutrition is one to which you must on no account give way. It could be fatal. The next thing is companionship. She's not well enough to have another animal in with her and, as you know, donkeys aren't over-fond of strange dogs. So, for the first few days, I'd like people—you and Chrissie, of course—and anyone else available to come and talk to her, giving her love and encouragement.'

'Lucky that she's a jenny,' Joanna said, and Paul nodded. 'I know what you mean. Not so likely to have psychological problems. A male could easily turn vicious as a result of this neglect.'

The new arrival was a source of compassionate interest to everyone and Liz said, 'I'll stay with her for a while instead of going home.'

'Well, you'll have company,' Joanna glanced down the yard, 'Clare's coming.'

Petting and talking to the donkey, Clare seemed oblivious to all else for a few minutes, then suddenly she turned, went up to Paul and engaged him in conversation. Glancing across at them, Joanna saw Paul take out his diary and write something down—something that evidently pleased Clare. She was smiling and pleasant when, a few minutes later, she followed Joanna into the surgery. Standing at the office door, she said,

'Paul is absolutely right to give that donkey a chance of life. He says he's going to explore the possibility of getting her into a donkey sanctuary when the farrier has done his work on her feet. He told me he was going down to Suffolk to see his parents this weekend, but instead he's going down to visit a sanctuary in this area. I asked if I could go with him and he agreed so long as I wouldn't find it too boring. Boring!—why, I'm thrilled!'

Joanna made the right comments, but as soon as Clare had shut the door, she went into the dispensary and stood for a while staring unseeingly at the rows of bottles. Trying to analyse the depression sweeping over her, she realised that it was mainly a question of hurt pride. Paul had rejected her company in favour of that of Clare, but what did it matter? Quickly she conquered her feeling of resentment and smiled wryly at her foolishness. The less she saw of Paul the better for her own peace of mind. There seemed to be a kind of antipathy between them that was difficult to explain—a clash of personality that made her uneasy. Glancing at her watch, she decided to go up to her flat, but at that moment the door opened and Paul came in.

'I've been thinking,' he said abruptly, 'would you like to come to the donkey sanctuary after all? Clare is coming and I'm sure she's like you to join us.'

CHAPTER FOUR

FOR A MOMENT Joanna stood stunned into silence. Then, suddenly, she was filled with resentment. He already regrets having agreed to Clare's request, she thought angrily, and he's just making use of me in order to keep her at a distance.

'I can't possibly manage it,' she said stiffly, then added a little maliciously, 'In any case, two's company, you know—or is that what you're afraid of?'

His mouth tightened. 'What a charming way in which to decline an invitation! I should have known better than to ask you, of course. I've already gathered that I'm a crashing bore, and now it seems that I'm devious into the bargain.' He paused and his eyes were so full of anger that she flinched involuntarily. 'Sandy said you were the iceberg type and he found that exciting. Well, I don't like icebergs. Beautiful, yes—but frigid and hard as hell.'

Cheeks scarlet and blinking hard to hold back furious tears, Joanna's face gave the lie to his harsh description, but before she could find a suitable retort, he had gone. From the office she could hear Clare speaking on the telephone and realised thankfully that Paul's taunting sneers had not been overheard. With her heart still beating fast she took refuge up in her flat and, over coffee and a sandwich, she gradually grew calmer. It was what she wanted, wasn't it? Her refusal to get involved with anyone was bound to lead to this kind of criticism. 'Frigid—hard as hell'—hurtful words, but she must let them stand. Better to be coldly aloof than to be like Clare, flinging herself at every man who came her way. And if, to ease her conscience, Clare confessed to Paul what she had done to him, she would be making a terrible mistake. Merciless and implacable, he would be so savagely contemptuous that she would be devastated. Then, no doubt, she would revert to her former unpleasant self and make life difficult in the surgery.

Suddenly, black depression swept over Joanna. This new job was turning out to be full of tension and misunderstanding. Somehow she must find a way of escape. But how? What could she do in a strange environment with no friends and no outside interests? Normally one would expect to find someone congenial in a practice of this size, but they all seemed to have problems in which she had no wish to get entangled. Liz was the only one who seemed untroubled at the moment, but that could change any day. Better to look outside for her relaxation—get right away from the veterinary profession. Perhaps Mrs Holman might have some ideas on the subject, she was so kindly and motherly that it might be a good thing to confide in her.

Joanna's mood lightened as she finished her coffee. When the opportunity presented itself she would unburden herself to the junior partner's wife and maybe she would receive some constructive advice. Glancing at her watch, she saw that there was time to spare before afternoon surgery—time to go out and have a look at the local shops.

Opening the small door alongside the big gates leading into the yard, she stood for a moment undecided as to which direction to take. Then, suddenly, she heard a loud, protesting miaow so near to her feet that it made her jump. Glancing down quickly she saw a closed cardboard carton standing against the wall. Lifting it carefully, she read the scrawled message on the lid, and frowned. No shopping today. This was more important.

Before opening the carton she went into the office and told Clare.

'Of all the heartless things to do——!' Clare read the message aloud. ' ''Please put this cat to sleep. We don't want her any more.'' Poor thing—I suppose she's old and dirty.'

Pulling on her gloves, Joanna opened the lid and grasped the scruff of the loudly protesting inmate.

'No—look, she's quite young. About three-quarters grown, I should say. A nice tabby.'

The cat showed no inclination to scratch as she cradled it in her arms and Clare said,

'She'd be beautiful if she weren't so terribly thin. Pretty markings and lots of white. What a shame to throw her out like that.' She hesitated. 'What—what do you think? Will you——?'

Joanna looked thoughtful, then, handing the cat to Clare, she went into the dispensary, filled a saucer with milk and placed it on the floor. The two girls watched in silence as the pink tongue shot out eagerly and the milk rapidly disappeared. Purring now, the tabby submitted quietly to Joanna's examination and, eventually looking up, she said,

'Nothing wrong that I can see. She seems absolutely healthy. Well, I'm not going to put her to sleep, that's for sure.' She paused. 'I'll keep her.'

Clare sighed with relief. 'Thank goodness! If you hadn't said it first I was going to offer, but your need is probably greater than mine. She'll be great company for you in your flat.'

Joanna nodded thoughtfully. 'I know if an owner demands that an animal be put to sleep a vet is ethically bound to do so, but this case is different. The owner has abandoned the cat and there's no question of payment for putting it down, so——'

'Exactly,' Clare said approvingly. 'Oh, Joanna, you really love animals, don't you?'

'Of course. A fine kind of vet I'd be if I didn't.' Joanna picked up her new pet. 'Come on, puss. You look very hungry. I've got some bits and pieces upstairs that will tide you over till I can get some proper food for you.'

'I'll go out now and get some,' Clare said, then giving a final stroke to the tabby, she asked, 'Has she been spayed?'

'No. I'll have to do her later when she's settled down.'

Clare laughed and tickled the cat under the chin. 'All kinds of treats in store for you, puss. Injections, worming and finally a spay! You don't know how lucky you are to be taken on as a vet's pet.' She paused. ' "Lucky"! That should be her name.'

Joanna laughed. 'Very appropriate! Come on then, Lucky, and I'll show you your new home.'

She was halfway up the stairs when the outer door opened and she heard Chrissie's voice. Standing still for a moment she listened apprehensively but, to her relief, the conversation sounded friendly. Clare was evidently recounting the event of the morning. Perhaps now the two girls would get on better. Harmony in the surgery would make life easier all round.

Lucky settled down remarkably well. She seemed almost touchingly grateful for the loving care and good diet her new mistress lavished on her. Very talkative, constantly purring, she showed her affection by jumping on Joanna's lap and gently patting her face with a velvety paw. When left alone she settled down on a sunny windowsill, gazing down with interest on the comings and goings in the yard below.

Soon the day came when Joanna decided she must spay her cat so that eventually she could be allowed outside. With Liz helping, Lucky was quickly anaesthesised, then Joanna clipped and shaved a square area of her left flank. Sterile cloths were placed around the operation site, then Liz handed over a small, sharp-bladed scalpel with which Joanna made the incisions through the skin and muscle layers. Searching expertly, she found the small uterus and one horn attached to the ovary. Artery forceps were fixed on the far side, then she tied off and cut. She did the same thing with the other horn, then put two artery forceps over the base of the uterus, cut in between, tied off, then cut above the tie. One suture in the muscle and two in the skin and the operation was complete. Standing back from the table, Joanna met Liz's admiring gaze.

'I've never seen that done so quickly,' she said. 'I'm most impressed.' Placing Lucky in a recovery cage, she added, 'I won't have coffee now. The farrier is coming at eleven and I'd like to watch him at work on the donkey. How about coming along?'

Joanna hesitated. 'No—I don't think so. I'd like to stay and watch Lucky. She should begin to shiver in about half an hour.' It was a good excuse, she thought. There was always the possibility that Paul would be with the farrier if he could fit it in with his calls and for the last few days she managed to avoid him. Going into the dispensary, she put on the kettle and a moment later Clare came out of the office.'

'How's Lucky? Coming round yet?'

'No, not yet. I gave her a long-acting anaesthetic so that she won't feel any pain afterwards. She'll begin to shiver soon, but she won't be properly round for another six to eight hours. Would you like some coffee?'

They were sitting at the table when suddenly the door opened and, to Joanna's dismay, Paul came in and Clare said,

'You timed that nicely. I'll get you a mug.'

To Joanna's annoyance he accepted the offer, then turning to her, he said calmly,

'I was out early this morning on a calving case at Clayton Farm and Mrs Clayton would like you to call this afteroon to look at the bitch you did the Caesar on. It's a bit off colour.

Joanna stared. 'Why didn't you look at it yourself?'

'Not my patient,' he said shortly. 'Of course if it had been urgent I would have, but from Mrs Clayton's description of the symptoms it wasn't necessary.'

'Clayton Farm,' Clare came back with Paul's coffee, 'do you know how to get there, Joanna?'

'No problem,' Paul said coolly, 'I have to go out there after lunch to have another look at the calf. I'll take you and bring you back in time for evening surgery.' He smiled sardonically. 'Save on the firm's petrol.'

'Very praiseworthy,' Joanna said drily. 'All the same, I'd rather go on my own. You might have another call out that way and then I'd be back late.'

'I don't anticipate anything.' Paul's mouth twitched at the corner. 'In any case, Clare can always send someone else. She's expert at that.'

Clare grimaced. 'Don't rub it in! I've improved a lot lately. Surely you've noticed it.' She glanced at him provocatively. 'I don't want to risk you changing your mind about taking me to the donkey sanctuary at the weekend.'

Paul gulped down his coffee and rose from the table. 'I'm not taking you,' he said acidly. 'You asked to come. A very different matter.' He stood for a moment gazing down mockingly at the two girls. 'One asked herself and the other refused my invitation!' He went to the door. 'I must get back to the donkey. I'll fetch you after lunch, Joanna.'

He was gone before Joanna could protest and Clare said indignantly, 'There are times when I hate that man.' Then, glancing quickly at Joanna, she asked, 'What did he mean—"the other refused my invitation"? Did he ask you to go with him to the donkey sanctuary?'

Joanna hesitated for a moment, then shrugged. 'Well, only when he had agreed to your request. I expect he thought there was safety in numbers.'

Clare frowned. 'You're nearly as cynical as he is! All the same, I'm glad you refused, because I shall take the opportunity to own up about——'

'Don't be so stupid,' Joanna interrupted violently. 'I've told you what I think about that. Why don't you leave well alone?'

'Because it's not well and I can't live with myself.'

To Joanna's dismay she saw that Clare was close to tears and for a few minutes she said nothing. Then, suddenly, curiosity overcame her.

'What actually did you do that was so terrible?' she asked lightly.

Clare shook her head and, after waiting a few seconds, Joanna got up from the table. Then, looking up quickly, Clare burst out: 'Oh, all right, I'll tell you.' She paused, biting her lip, then she said slowly, 'Paul was obviously obsessed with another girl and I was as jealous as hell because at that time I thought I was in love with him. So I thought up a scheme to break up the affair and when Paul happened to be alone with me one day in the surgery I brought the conversation round to Fiona. It wasn't difficult. He was only too glad to talk about her, and I was her best friend. Gradually I made him feel uneasy by implying that she had spoken to me about him in a way that wasn't altogether favourable. I got him really worried. So much so that, at last, he said he simply had to know what she felt about him and that if I didn't tell him he would do something desperate. I didn't quite know what he meant by that, but I didn't want him to go straight to Fiona and tell her what I had said. So I bound him to strict secrecy and finally I said reluctantly, 'It's only that she says she finds you boring at times. Especially when you go on about animals. She says she gets fed up with veterinary talk and only pretends to be interested because she hasn't got any other boyfriend at the moment.' Clare frowned. 'It was a downright lie, of course, because Fiona had told me herself that she was fascinated by the veterinary life and enthralled by Paul's conversation.'

Shocked and disgusted, Joanna was speechless for a few moments. Then, controlling her revulsion, she said carefully, 'But didn't Paul give Fiona the benefit of the doubt and ask her outright if it was true?'

Clare shook her head. 'No, he never got round to it because shortly afterwards Fiona, obviously upset, asked me if I had any idea why Paul had suddenly become so

cold towards her. Of course I said I hadn't a clue except
that—' Clare's voice shook and she looked at the ground,
'well, I went even further and told her that that kind of
behaviour was typical of him. He always showed when he
was getting bored with girls—that was how he finished
with them. And that, naturally, was why she went off
him.' Getting up, Clare walked restlessly about the room,
then suddenly, she turned and looked steadily at Joanna.
'You're horrified, aren't you? I can see it in your eyes.
Well, perhaps now you can see why I must make a clean
breast of it.'

Joanna pulled herself together. 'I understand that your
conscience is giving you hell and you feel that you can't
endure it much longer. But—' she drew a long
breath—'apart from easing your mind, will it do any
good?'

'Probably not. Fiona is married now. But I shall feel
better.'

And Paul will feel worse, thought Joanna. Still, it's no
affair of mine. 'You must do what you think best,' she
said at last, 'but I think you're being unnecessarily cruel.'

'Cruel? I don't see that,' Clare looked indignant.
'Surely it's better to tell the truth?'

Joanna opened her mouth, then shut it again and
Clare, reading her unspoken rebuke, turned scarlet and
went silently into the office just as Liz re-entered the
room.

'The farrier is a bit more hopeful,' she announced.
'he's done a lot of good work on those awful feet and
Jenny was so docile and good. She responds pathetically
to anyone who goes to keep her company. I'd love to give
her more food, but Paul is adamant on that subject, so I
suppose he's right.'

'I'm sure he is,' Joanna said firmly. 'It would be very
dangerous to over-feed her and could even be fatal. The
build-up must be very gradual.'

She picked up the appointments book, searching

carefully to see if she could find anyone who wanted a house call that afternoon in order to make that an excuse for going to the Claytons' farm in her own car. At last, with a small sigh, she shut the book. She would have to go with Paul—albeit reluctantly. But in order to avoid friction she would keep the conversation strictly professional. Suddenly her mind went back to the accusation he had flung at her in that last row and the way in which he had reacted. He had said that it was obvious she found him boring and devious into the bargain. Boring—that was the operative word. Clare had told him Fiona found his conversation boring, and she herself had implied as much when he had talked so enthusiastically about Suffolk. That was the chip on his shoulder. His male pride was hurt. No man liked to be thought a bore. But it wasn't true. In Fiona's case it was a lie and in her own case he had jumped to the wrong conclusion. There was nothing, however, that she could do about it, it was all too involved.

After a quick snack Joanna went downstairs just as Chrissie arrived and after telling her where she could be found in case of an emergency she went outside to wait for Paul. If, she reflected, he were late, she would have the satisfaction of pointing out to him that it would have been better if she had gone on her own. In fact—she glanced at her watch—I'll give him ten minutes, then I'll get my car out, she thought. But even as she made her decision, he drove into the yard.

Leaning over to open the passenger door, he said, 'Just made it. I was afraid you would be setting off alone.'

She settled down and pulled the door to with a bang. 'I rather wish I had,' she said coldly. 'I think it's a bit demeaning to be taken along with you—just as though I were not a vet in my own right.'

'I never thought of that,' his voice was mildly sarcastic, 'but then I'm not constantly on the defensive like you women.'

Oh, dear, she thought ruefully, here we go again! She would very much like to refute his provocative statement, but the resultant argument would inevitably become deeply personal and therefore to be avoided at all costs. Shrugging indifferently, she felt she had made the point that his opinion was of no importance, but her satisfaction was shortlived.

He laughed shortly. 'So you won't rise to the bait?'

'No. I see no point in sexist statements like that. They're best ignored,' she retorted. Gazing ahead, she asked calmly, 'Is that the farm over there?'

'No. It's about four miles farther on. That's Greenlands Farm. Mr Harrison—he goes in for Jerseys. Lovely little creatures. A very rich client but a bad payer.'

They drove for a short time in silence until, suddenly a long sigh came unexpectedly from the back of the car, causing Joanna to turn round in astonishment.

'It's all right. Only Ben—my old springer spaniel. Very old, I'm sorry to say. He's fourteen.'

'Oh dear!' Joanna reached over to stroke the liver and white coat. Velvety eyes, sadly dimmed, gazed back at her and a thick, feathery tail lifted in friendly recognition of her sympathetic touch. 'Oh dear,' she said again, 'how sad for you, knowing that soon——' She stopped as, glancing quickly at Paul, she saw him wince.

He said nothing for a moment, then, swallowing hard, he spoke slowly. 'It hurts so much I daren't think about it. He's still happy, so I let him go on, but he grows weaker every day. I'm just hoping he'll die in his sleep. If he showed the slightest hint of suffering then of course I'd——' He stopped and drew a long, hard breath. 'It's hell when you have to put your own dog to sleep, but I wouldn't let anyone else do it.'

Tears came into Joanna's eyes. 'I know—oh, I do know. I had to do it to our old family Labrador a few months ago. It still hurts, even now.'

He turned to glance at her. 'Tears,' he said quietly. 'So

you have got a heart after all.'

An indignant retort was on the tip of her tongue, but she managed to hold it back. Instead she said softly, 'Oh, yes. It's a bit bruised, but——'

She broke off abruptly biting her lip, then tried to cover up. 'What I mean is——' then she stopped again as Paul turned the car suddenly off the main road into a narrow track leading up th farm buildings, and, thankfully, she relapsed into silence. Perhaps, she thought hopefully, he didn't hear her unintentional self-betrayal, but her hopes were dashed when, pulling up in order to get out and open the farm gate, he turned and gave her a long, brooding look.

Hurriedly she opened the passenger door and went straight over to the farmhouse, leaving Paul to pull on his boots and his obstetric gown.

The Border collie was lying in a warm bed in the kitchen and going down on her knees beside her, Joanna took her temperature.

'Yes,' she said at alst, 'it's up a bit—a hundred and two.'

'Oh dear!' Mrs Clayton looked worried, 'that's quite high.'

'No, not really. Normal for a dog is a hundred and one and a half, but it would go up higher without treatment and then she could lose her milk. I'll give her an injection now and tablets for three times a day beginning tomorrow. She should be OK in about three days!' 'But what is it?' Mrs Clayton was still troubled. 'It can't be a chill—I've kept her warm all the time. I've really been very careful.'

'Post-parturient fever. It happens sometimes after a Caesarian. Don't worry. She'll be all right. Antibiotics are live-savers,' Joanna said calmly. 'You were right to call me in.' The injection given and the tablets doled out, she asked, 'What are you going to do with the puppies?'

'We're going to keep the bitch ourselves and a friend of

ours wants the dog, so no problem there.' Mrs Clayton
brightened up. 'A new puppy and a new calf. It's a nice
little heifer, thanks to Mr Copeland. It was a difficult
calving, but he was so good and patient. My husband
wanted to drag the calf out with a rope on the back of a
tractor, but Mr Copeland would have none of that. He
said the calf was lying badly and he spent over an hour
straightening it out. Then she came quite easily. He
doesn't seem to mind what he goes through—his right
arm was very bruised, squeezed hard with every
contraction—but he only laughed.' Mrs Clayton paused
for breath, then, glancing out of the window, she said,
'Here they come. Just in time for a cup of tea.'

Mr Clayton strode into the kitchen and pulled out a
chair for Paul. 'Don't tell me you've got to get away
immediately,' he said jovially. 'My wife has got one of her
fruit cakes out. That's an honour for you. She doesn't cut
into one for the doctor—perhaps she's afraid he'll start
talking about calories, but you and I know that a bit of
homemade cake won't do you any harm after using up so
many calories while struggling with a temperamental
cow.' He grinned at Joanna. 'That's not the sort of work
for you, is it, miss? You're better with the cats and dogs, I
expect.'

Mrs Clayton nodded in agreement, but Joanna felt a
twinge of irritation. 'Women vets can deal with large
animals too, you know,' she said crisply. 'We all have the
same training.' She paused as Mr Clayton pursed his lips.
'I'll admit that a difficult calving calls for a lot of physical
strength but, on the whole, we can cope quite well.'

Mrs Clayton smiled as her husband looked doubtful.
'You'd have to wait a long time before the average farmer
would call you in instead of a male vet. Very conservative
farmers are—stuck in their own mud, you could say.' She
laughed heartily at her own wit, then she added, 'Talking
of small animals reminds me: our son Peter has a tortoise.
He's had it since last May, but now he's worried because

it seems to have stopped eating and doesn't move about much. His father says it's on the way out and Peter is very upset. Would one of you mind having a look at it?' She paused, glancing at Joanna. 'Does that come under the heading of small animals?'

Joanna nodded. 'I expect it's beginning to think about hibernating for the winter. Where does Peter keep it?'

'Well, usually it lives in the shed out there. The door stays open so it can get out when it wants, but since he's seemed so poorly Peter has brought it indoors. It's there in the scullery.'

Joanna got up and went into the old-fashioned scullery where in a box by the oil-fired boiler reposed a very lethargic tortoise.

'He looks a bit better,' said Mrs Clayton. 'I expect it's being in here. It's lovely and warm for him. Look, he's moving around—perhaps there's nothing wrong with him after all.'

'There will be if you stop him going into hibernation, which is what he wants to do. It's far too hot in here for him. I'll tell you what he needs. A nice cool place—a large box with plenty of straw in—that shed you told me about would be ideal. And he should be left quite undisturbed. I think an injection of multi-vitamins would be a good thing—it would help him survive the winter.'

Mr Clayton laughed as she went back into the kitchen to fetch her case. 'That's a new one on me. Injecting a tortoise! How will you do it? Hammer it through his shell?'

Joanna filled a syringe. 'His back leg is the place,' she said calmly, and a few seconds later she suited the action to her words. 'There you are, and the sooner you're out in the shed the better.'

As they got into the car and waved goodbye Paul chuckled softly. 'I think you impressed Mr Clayton, though rather against his will. He's a real male chauvinist, isn't he?'

'Most men are,' said Joanna coolly. 'It's only natural, I suppose. After centuries of thinking themselves superior to women it must be hard for them to change their ideas.' She smiled wryly. 'With men like Mr Clayton physical strength is more important than brains. With others it's beauty that counts more than anything.'

'A scathing generalisation,' Paul's voice was sardonic. 'A real man-hater, aren't you?'

'So would you be if——' Joanna broke off quickly, horrified at her impulsive reaction to his mockery. Closing her lips tightly, she turned to stare out of the side window.

'Well, well!' Paul glanced at her curiously but said no more, and the silence lasted for the rest of the journey. Then when he pulled up outside the gates into the yard he said,

'I'm going down to see the donkey. Are you coming?'

Joanna hesitated. 'No, not just now. I must look at a patient I operated on this morning.'

His eyebrows rose quizzically. 'Chrissie is there, isn't she?' He paused. 'Really, Joanna,' he added bitingly, 'you do make the most feeble excuses. Why don't you just say outright that you've had enough of my company for one afternoon?'

Irritated, Joanna drew a long breath. 'Paul Copeland, I think you're the most disagreeable man I've ever met! You have a tongue like a viper!'

He stared at her grimly for a moment then, getting out, he went to open the gates. As soon as the car was in the yard Joanna opened the passenger door and left him without another word. With a momentary feeling of satisfaction she reflected on her small triumph. She had no reason to regret her words, she told herself. The only subjects they could discuss with any degree of cordiality were veterinary ones but as soon as the talk became general he seemed to have the knack of arousing all her animosity. He really was unbearable. A few more adjectives came into her mind. Arrogant, dictatorial, pompous and boring. Well, no. On second thoughts he was neither pompous nor boring. But exasperating to a degree that infuriated her. Her resolution to appear indifferent had been broken by her outburst of anger, but there was no harm in letting him know what she thought of him. Giving herself a mental pat on the back for having put him down so thoroughly, she went into the surgery and greeted Chrissie smilingly.

'How's Lucky?' She went over to the recovery cage and was met by a loud miaow as two huge green eyes gleamed at her indignantly.

Chrissie laughed. 'I think she realises that her life style has changed. She's come round very well. Still a bit wobbly, of course, but I gave her a little milk a short time ago and she lapped it up.' She paused. 'Did you enjoy your trip with Paul?'

'It was all right,' Joanna shrugged. 'There wasn't much wrong with the Border collie. She'll be OK in a day or two. Are there any messages?'

'Nothing for you. A dog was brought in with a cut foot. It was on the pad and you know how it bleeds. I thought the owner was going to faint, so I gave her a cup of tea when I'd dressed the cut and bandaged it.' Chrissie hesitated, then added slowly, 'Mark came in and I took my courage in both hands and asked if he would like to see that film I told you about.' She stopped for a moment, then burst out, 'Guess what? He said yes and we're going tomorrow evening!'

'Nice work,' Joanna smiled. 'I hope it all goes the way you want.'

'As to that, I've got my doubts.' Chrissie's pale face flushed painfully. 'Mark hasn't a clue how I feel about him.'

Joanna laughed. 'Chrissie, I'm not—repeat not—going to give you advice on how to proceed any further. You're on your own now.'

'Well, I'll let you know what happens anyway. That's if you're really interested in my love life.'

Joanna's first impulse was to say that she wasn't at all interested, but that would have been unkind, so she assured Chrissie that she would love to hear how she and Mark got on and left it at that.

But, later that evening, in the solitude of her flat she

reflected ruefully on the prospect of becoming a kind of agony aunt to Chrissie and Clare. How much nicer it would be if she herself had a confidante, someone to whom she could open her heart. She got up restlessly and went to the window, gazing unseeingly out on to the yard. Evening surgery was over. She had eaten a rather dull meal and here she was with absolutely nothing to do in her spare time.

As if to show her she was wrong the telephone rang, and she smiled wryly as she picked up the receiver, her eyes widened in astonishment as she listened. She said at last,

'Yes, I should love to come, Mrs Mayfield. Thank you for asking me.'

Then, after listening to further instructions, she put down the receiver with the pleasant feeling that things were looking up. Dinner with the Mayfields to meet the new vet who would be replacing Sandy Wilson. A small party, Mrs Mayfield had said. Ten in all—now who, she wondered, would they be? The Mayfields and Clare, the new vet and herself—that made five. Then of course the Holmans—three left. Her heart sank a little as the thought of Paul and Mark came into her mind. Naturally they would be invited as well, and that left one unknown. To make up the numbers correctly another woman was needed, so perhaps the new vet was married. Well, anyway, it was a beginning to her social life, though probably it wouldn't be very exciting as it was so obviously a purely veterinary affair. She went to her wardrobe and stood pondering. What to wear? That was a bit of a problem as her clothes were mostly practical. She searched for a while, then found two dresses from which to choose. She must have a word with Clare to find out just how formal a gathering it would be.

But Clare, when approached next morning, said any old dress would do and her mother apologised for giving such short notice, but the new vet was still working in his old practice and this evening was the only one he had free.

'I haven't met him yet,' she said, 'but I gather he's rather nice-looking and quite amusing. Let's hope he's an improvement on our present male staff.'

Surgery was quiet and with no operations to follow, Joanna refused coffee and went up to her flat to see how Lucky was doing. She had recovered very quickly and showed her affection for her new mistress by curling round Joanna's legs and purring loudly.

Picking her up and cuddling her, Joanna said aloud, 'It isn't fair to keep you cooped up here all day. I'll take you down into the yard so that you can get used to your new surroundings.'

Outside she put Lucky on the ground, knowing that as she was not yet back to her full strength there was no likelihood that she would attempt to climb the high wall and wander off. All was quiet in the yard, and with Lucky staying close to her she decided to go and visit the donkey.

Jenny was still looking mournful, but already the poor deformed feet showed the benefit of the farrier's work. It could only be a gradual improvement, however, and for a moment Joanna wondered if, after all, it would have been kinder to put her to sleep. But when she gently stroked the rough coat she felt a little shudder run through the thin back and suddenly the sad little creature pushed gently against her in a pathetic show of gratitude for her sympathy, a gesture that pulled at Joanna's heartstrings. Talking to her softly, she forgot Lucky for a moment until suddenly she realised that the cat had followed her into the loosebox and was purring round Jenny in unmistakable friendliness. Holding her breath, Joanna waited for Jenny's reaction, ready to pull Lucky away at the evidence of fear on the donkey's part. With her hand still on Jenny's back she could feel her suddenly stiffen, then, lowering her head, she began to examine the purring little cat. With her head turning this way and that she watched Lucky's movements with interest until, at last, Joanna bent down to pick up the cat. Lucky, however, had made up her mind and had no desire to leave her new friend. With a loud miaow she jumped up on a beam out of Joanna's reach and began washing her face, watched all the time by Jenny, whose dull eyes seemed perceptibly brighter.

Joanna hesitated. She could not stay there much longer, but Lucky quite obviously had no intention of leaving. At last Joanna moved away, calling as she did so, and then, looking back, she saw Lucky jump down and settle in a purring little heap beside Jenny as if to show that this was where she intended to spend the next few hours. And Jenny, touchingly, bent her head and gave Lucky a gentle, friendly nudge.

Joanna gazed at them thoughtfully. 'I haven't the heart to separate you,' she said aloud, then jumped as a voice behind her said approvingly, 'Quite right,' and she turned quickly to see Paul.

'I heard about the cat you'd adopted,' he said. 'Now I see she's adopted Jenny. The very thing she needs—an animal friend. It will help no end. What's your cat's name?'

Joanna told him, adding ruefully, 'But she's not answering to it right now. What do you think? Shall I leave her here?'

'Oh yes, please. The best kind of therapy for Jenny. You'd better put her food outside, though. Jenny is on a rigid diet at the moment.'

'Do you think Lucky has taken up her abode here permanently?'

Paul nodded. 'It looks like it, and I'm glad for Jenny's sake. I'm afraid you've lost your pet for the time being anyway.'

'What about when Jenny goes away? Do you think Lucky will pine?'

'Probably. But we'll cross that bridge when we come to it.' He paused. 'What do you think of Jenny's feet now?'

'Improved, certainly, but I doubt if they'll ever get right again.'

'Maybe not absolutely right, but she's very young and with regular trimming and a great deal of time and patience it may be possible to correct the angle of the hoof. Once she has established her new balance it may correct the tendons that have been so badly stretched. It can't be done suddenly—no question of operating—she would never stand the anaesthetic.' Paul stopped and frowned thoughtfully. 'I can't keep her here indefinitely, of course, so I can only hope the donkey sanctuary will take her in when she's recovered enough to be acceptable.'

Joanna glanced at her watch. 'I must go,' and she began to move away, then stopped and asked hesitatingly, 'By the way, I've been invited up to the Mayfields' to dinner this evening to meet the new vet. I suppose you and Mark will be there too.'

'Of course. Royal Command,' Paul shrugged. 'Not my favourite way of passing my spare time—these Mayfield dinners are very stiff and formal.'

'Oh dear!' Joanna looked dismayed. 'I asked Clare what I should wear and she said "any old thing".'

'A typical feminine trick, that,' Paul smiled sardonically, 'but don't worry. It's not dinner jacket for men or long dresses for the women.' He turned and gave her a long look that, much to her annoyance, caused her to flush. 'You'll look beautiful in anything—"any old thing", in fact.' He paused. 'When I said stiff and formal I meant the atmosphere. Mrs Mayfield is cold and distant and hasn't got a shred of humour in her. Mr Mayfield—well, he's all right, and you've met him already. Clare of course will be making a dead set at the new man and is probably afraid of competition from you.'

'Competition? Good heavens! If you imagine——'

'I don't imagine anything,' Paul said crisply, 'I know Clare.'

But did he? Probably not as well as he thought, Joanna mused wryly as she returned to the surgery. Clare's confession—if and when she made it to him—would be a shocking eye-opener. Evidence of such deceit was almost certain to make him even more cynical that he was already.

She frowned to herself as cruel memories came flooding back. She herself was a victim of deceit and it had had much the same effect on her. Perhaps that attitude accounted for the antagonism that seemed to flare up every now and then between Paul and herself. They were two of a kind really. Not that that made any difference. Paul and she would never be close friends. He was far too arrogant for a start. Too—suddenly she smiled ruefully. She was at it again—trying to find the most unpleasant adjectives to describe his character. So silly of her when actually she was endeavouring to put him right out of her mind.

Just before leaving that morning, Liz said suddenly, 'I hear you're going up to dinner at the Mayfields' tonight.'

Joanna stared. 'Now how on earth could you have heard so quickly?'

'Mark told me yesterday. He hates going up there. He says what with Mrs M's patronising manner and Clare trying to make it with the new vet it will be utterly boring. The only thing that will make it endurable for him is the fact that you'll be there.'

'Oh dear!' Joanna frowned. 'I hope he won't say that to Chrissie.'

'Well, she heard, I'm sure of that. We were down with the donkey—Chrissie had come in early to see her. I saw from her face that it hit her hard.' Liz paused. 'I know you're not interested in Mark, but that doesn't stop him from being interested in you.'

Joanna tried to laugh it off, but Liz's remark made her uneasy. So much so that she resolved to put Chrissie's mind at rest when she came in after lunch. Then suddenly her heart sank. Of course. This evening Mark and Chrissie were supposed to be going to the cinema. What bad luck for Chrissie! Obviously Mark would have to abandon that engagement in favour of the 'Royal Command' invitation. That alone was bad enough, but having let Chrissie overhear his silly remark about Joanna's presence making the evening endurable—that was disastrous. She sighed heavily. Such a lot of undercurrents in this practice, and she was being swept along with them against her will.

When Chrissie arrived after lunch she was inclined to be cool and reserved. At first it was impossible to talk because an emergency was brought in almost immediately. A small mongrel dog had had the foolhardy idea of attacking a Jack Russell terrier and had come out of the fight very much the worse for wear. The owner was highly indignant.

'All Billy did was to go into the garden where that Jack Russell lives and bark at him. Then he was immediately attacked. Ferocious—you never saw anything like the way that horrible dog came for him! If the owner hadn't managed to drag him away—well, I think Billy would have been killed. As it is, he's nearly torn to pieces.'

'Oh, it's not as bad as that.' Joanna finished examining the unlucky loser. 'There are one or two rather nasty bites which need a stitch or two, but I think he'll survive to fight another day. That is, if you can't manage to stop him going into other dogs' gardens.'

'He only barked at him,' the owner said defensively, then brightening up, she added, 'I've got the address, so will you send your bill in to them? I don't see why I should pay for an unprovoked attack.'

'But it wasn't unprovoked.' Joanna stood waiting for the local anaesthetic to take effect. 'Your dog went uninvited into a private garden and the Jack Russell defended his territory.' She took the suturing needle from Chrissie. 'I'm afraid you'll have to pay for this treatment. After that, it's up to you to try and recover the money, but I don't think you've got a hope. You'll just have to train your Billy not to stray into private gardens.'

'Oh, he's too independent for that. He's very strong-willed.' The owner seemed almost proud of her own subordination to her pet. When, after a certain amount of argument as to the amount charged for the treatment, the ineffectual lady was dragged out by her troublesome pet, Joanna looked at Chrissie and shrugged resignedly.

'No doubt as to who's boss in that household?' she said wryly, then frowned as Chrissie turned away indifferently. Impulsively she said quickly, 'Look—I know you must be upset because Mark has to put off your date for the cinema, but he couldn't refuse to go to the Mayfields' dinner party, could he?'

'Of course he could!' Chrissie turned, her eyes blazing in her pale face. 'At such short notice anyone would be justified in pleading another engagement.'

'Yes—I suppose so,' Joanna said carefully, 'but the film goes on for another two days. Can't you go then?'

Chrissie shook her head miserably. 'I did suggest it, but Mark said he wouldn't be free.' She paused, then added reluctantly, 'the truth is he's more interested in you than in me.'

'Oh, what nonsense! I don't believe it. In any case I've told you before that I'm not interested in getting involved with anyone here. Why don't you believe me?'

'You could change your mind at any time, couldn't you?' Chrissie gave a twisted smile. 'Oh, I know—it's not your fault if Mark fancies you. Just my bad luck, I suppose.'

Joanna said no more but made a mental resolve to try and find out from Mark himself what he really thought about Chrissie. It would have to be done very tactfully. Perhaps the dinner party would provide the necessary opportunity. Also it was important that Mark in turn, should know how Chrissie felt about him. He was almost bound to feel flattered, and flattery, Joanna told herself a little cynically, was a sure way of arousing a man's interest.

Immediately after evening surgery Joanna went up to her flat, had a long relaxing bath, washed her hair, then stood gazing into her wardrobe, still undecided as to which of her two dresses she would wear. Almost reluctantly, she pulled out the one in which she knew she looked her best. Soft almond green in very fine wool, she had worn it last autumn, but it was so beautifully cut that it could never be dated. A wide leather belt so supple that it was like a sash emphasised her slim waist, the boat-shaped neck showed up her glowing skin and with her shining dark hair falling in a deep wave on to her shoulders she knew without vanity that she looked a vision of beauty. Knew, because James had told her so. He had loved the dress, had called her the Aphrodite of the North Sea when she had worn it for the first and only time just before—she shuddered and drew her hand across her eyes as the bitter memories flooded back. She ought never to have kept such a poignant reminder of the past.

Glancing at her watch, she saw it was time to leave. Time to attend the 'Royal Command' dinner that was said to be so dreary. Surely it couldn't be as bad as all that? Better to put the doleful prophecy out of her mind and try to enjoy herself on this her first social gathering in her new job.

CHAPTER FIVE

THE PROPHECY, however, seemed at first to be only too accurate. Mrs Mayfield welcomed Joanna formally, saw to it that she was provided with a drink, then left her to circulate among the company. Gazing with interest round the room, Joanna decided that it reflected her hostess's character. Beautifully furnished, rich curtains, expensive rugs on polished floors—somehow it was stiff and impersonal. Perhaps, she reflected, that atmosphere accounted for Clare's rebellious disposition.

Her thoughts were interrupted by Mr Mayfield who came forward to greet her. 'I hear,' he said smilingly, 'that you've been very kind to my difficult daughter.'

He nodded to where Clare stood in the centre of the room talking to Mark and two other men, one of whom Joanna guessed must be the new vet.

'Difficult?' she shrugged. 'Well, perhaps she is sometimes, but it's probably because she's a bit lonely. She doesn't make friends easily.'

Mr Mayfield nodded rather sadly. 'Yes, that's true, but she's very mixed-up in herself. She doesn't seem to know what she wants to do with her life.'

Joanna looked at him sympathetically. His thin face showed real concern for his daughter. Impulsively she said, 'Clare is very fond of animals, but she's out of place in a veterinary practice. I should have thought she could have found her happiness in another line. Something to do with animal welfare perhaps——' she broke off as she saw Clare approaching. Mr Mayfield nodded thoughtfully as he went off to another group of guests and, as Clare came up, she said,

'Joanna, meet Freddy Conway—our new vet,' she turned to the man beside her. 'Freddy, Joanna is in charge of the small animal side of our practice. You'll have to mind your ps and qs with her. She doesn't stand any nonsense from anyone.'

'Oh dear!' Joanna smiled ruefully as she shook hands. 'Clare, you're making me out to be an absolute tyrant!'

'I'm sure you're not that,' Freddy Conway grinned at her cheerfully, and Joanna warmed to his friendliness. Hazel eyes under a shock of thick fair hair, athletic-looking, his pleasant face healthily tanned, he was very attractive.

Clare, quite obviously, found that too. Seeing his immediate interest in Joanna, she frowned slightly, then turned quickly to the other man beside her. 'And here is Dr Andrew Porter. He's just come to join Mr Ferguson's practice. I'll leave you two to fight it out,' she said over her shoulder, and led Freddy Conway firmly away.

'Well, that sounds a bit ominous,' Andrew Porter laughed as he shook hands. 'What can she mean by that? Do I look the aggressive type?'

Joanna laughed as she studied him. Medium height, brown wavy, well groomed hair, brown eyes and a sensitive mouth in a thin, serious face, a kind, sympathetic doctor, she decided. 'Perhaps she means that our two professions will lead to medical arguments, but I don't think that's likely, do you?'

'Far from it. I wouldn't dare to argue with a veterinary surgeon. For one thing, I'm not a surgeon. A very ordinary GP, that's me. As for medical talk—well, yes. Your veterinary work fascinates me. The variety—your methods of diagnosis—no help at all from your patients. We doctors deal only with male and female humans, whereas you have all those different species with totally different anatomies——' he paused, his brown eyes warm with interest. 'And to see such erudition allied to such feminine beauty—well, I'm full of admiration.' He watched appreciatively as the colour rose in her cheeks, then he said, 'Don't you think it would be a very good idea if you came out to dinner with me one evening soon so that we could compare our work?'

Joanna's eyes widened in astonishment at such a speedy invitation and Andrew grinned disarmingly. 'I don't believe in wasting time—how about it?'

For a moment Joanna hesitated, then she smiled back at him. 'That would be very nice,' she said demurely, and felt a glow of pleasure when he said quickly,

'Right. Tomorrow evening—that's if you're free.'

She nodded, determined that she would indeed be free, then suddenly she flushed again, her eyes on someone behind Andrew.

'Good evening, Joanna, I see you found the perfect dress after all. I must say you look more like a glamorous model than a veterinary surgeon.' Paul turned quickly as Mark joined them. 'Ah, here's another admirer,' then he added laughing as he moved away, 'Good luck, doctor. You'll need it. The competition is fierce, you know.'

Controlling with difficulty a strong urge to throw the contents of her glass at him, Joanna felt her irritation increase as Mark said in an undertone,

'May I have a word with you, Joanna?'

With a quick lift of his eyebrows Andrew shrugged lightly and turned away, leaving Joanna frowning resentfully at Mark. Impatiently she said, 'What's so important that it can't wait till later?'

'Don't look so cross.' He hesitated, then added apologetically, 'I'm sorry if I broke up an interesting conversation, but in view of the-er-competition I thought I'd better jump in quickly. I wanted to ask you if you'd like to come to the cinema with me tomorrow evening. There's a good film on about Africa—lots of animals—should be interesting.'

Joanna blinked in astonishment, then, with a sharp pang of pity for Chrissie, she said shortly, 'Sorry, Mark, I can't manage it.' She paused. 'In any case, I thought you were going with Chrissie.'

'Oh—well,' he flushed guiltily, 'actually we were supposed to be going this evening, but of course this party' he shrugged and glanced round the room—'this had to take precedence.'

'Poor Chrissie,' Joanna said feelingly, 'she was so happy at the thought of going with you. She'd be terribly hurt if she knew you'd asked me instead.' To her surprise she saw that Mark was genuinely astonished and thought scornfully how imperceptive he was. Impulsively she added, 'Don't you know how she feels about you?'

Slowly his flush grew deeper. 'Feels about me? Chrissie? Good lord! I assure you, Joanna, I'd no idea——Are you sure? I mean, she's never given a sign——'

Half amused, half pityingly Joanna watched his face and saw that he was considerably shaken. He stood staring at her, obviously trying to come to grips with the startling idea that he was secretly loved by a girl he had taken very much for granted.

'Chrissie is a lovely girl and—' Joanna looked at Mark steadily, 'she thinks you're wonderful.'

Leaving him gazing thoughtfully into his glass, she moved around from group to group until it was time to go into dinner. Then, to her dismay, she found that she was placed next to Paul with the doctor on her other side.

Andrew Porter looked pleased as he laid his table napkin across his knees. 'This is a bit of luck. You'll be able to save me from feeling like a fish out of water.' He smiled at her. 'Yes, I know you're a vet too but, being a woman, you're bound to have other topics of conversation.'

She laughed and, as they joked and chatted through the first course, she almost forgot Paul who was quietly listening to Mrs Holman on his other side. Opposite to them Clare sat next to the new vet and was obviously in her element. Wearing a royal blue dress that showed off her slender figure, her blonde hair glowing under the light, she looked very pretty and her usual sullen mouth was warmly smiling.

At last Andrew turned to Mrs Mayfield and Joanna realised that Paul was saying something to her. 'I'm sorry,' she said stiffly, 'what did you say?'

He smiled sardonically. 'Nothing important. Were you dreaming of a new romance?'

'Don't be absurd,' she said derisively. 'You do say the most foolish things, you know.'

He laughed. 'Maybe. Well, now I'll be sensible. How about coming out with me tomorrow night? I know a very nice place where we could have an excellent dinner. Will you bury the hatchet and come?'

Her fork halfway to her mouth, she stared at him for a long moment. Then putting it down again she said very deliberately, 'Thank you for asking me, but tomorrow night I'm going out with Andrew.'

'Andrew?' His eyes looked beyond her to the doctor on her other side. 'Good lord! You're a fast worker, aren't you?'

'Nothing to do with me,' she returned mockingly. 'He says he doesn't believe in wasting time. He's very amusing.'

'Ah, well,' Paul's eyes glinted as he glanced once more at the doctor, 'we'll have to make it another time. How about Friday?'

Joanna's smile was cold. 'No, thank you, Paul. Not Friday or any other day.'

His face flushed, but just as he was about to speak, Mark, on the other side of Clare, gave a quiet chuckle. Leaning across the table, he said, 'Hard luck, Paul. I've been brushed off too. Joanna declined my offer of a visit to the cinema in much the same way.'

Paul's flush faded, leaving his face very pale. Then he turned abruptly to Mrs Holman and, for the rest of the meal, he ignored Joanna completely.

Driving home, Joanna felt a glow of satisfaction. On the whole a successful evening, she reflected. She had managed to put Paul in his place, done what she could for Chrissie and found a friend quite unconnected with her work. It would be fun to go out with Andrew. His frank admiration was pleasing, he was undeniably attractive and, just so long as he remained only a friend, she would be content. Instinctively she knew that she did not want any more than friendship. She was not yet ready for anything emotional. Luckily, she reflected, Andrew didn't stir her pulses and somehow she knew he never would. But it was a beginning to a social life outside the practice, and that was what she wanted more than anything.

Next morning she looked at the list for her time off and found, to her relief, that she had been right in saying she was free for that evening. All the same, to be on the safe side she would find out from Andrew where they were going in order to leave a telephone number in case of an emergency. The surgery that morning was busy, but most of the cases were routine until about eleven Joanna was called to the telephone.

'It's Paul—' Liz held out the receiver, 'he wants to speak to you.'

Anticipating trouble, Joanna frowned, but after listening for a short while she said enthusiastically, 'Oh yes, it will be very interesting. As soon as possible? Well, surgery is just about finished and I haven't any operations this morning, so come right along.'

Putting down the receiver, she turned to Liz. 'What do you know? Paul wants to do an entropion on a young—five or six month old tigress. Apparently he attends a small private zoo and they haven't any hospital facilities, so he's going to do it here. In about half an hour, he says.'

'That's the zoo out at Waybourne,' Liz said. 'It's not

very big—I didn't know they had any tigers.'

'Paul says it's a new venture for them. They've bought four tiger cubs and one of the females has the entropion. Paul wants to do the operation, so I'll do the anaesthetising. Let's get everything ready before we have coffee.'

They were just finishing when Clare, who had joined them, looked out of the window. 'Here they come—the keeper has got it on a lead. It looks absolutely adorable—enormous big paws—it seems quite tame.'

Paul came in first and said quickly, 'I know she looks sweet and cuddly, but keep your distance. Chloe is very, very strong and she's not too keen on strangers.'

The young tigress was about three feet tall with a long, lithe body. But the beautiful face was marred by a deformation of the left eye. Discoloured and watery, the eyelid was curled up into the eye itself, causing constant irritation from the lashes rubbing against the eyeball. Gently the two men lifted her on to the already lowered table and the keeper stroked her soothingly while it was slowly raised to the correct height. Then Paul said,

'You'd better continue to hold her while Miss Bramford and I give the anaesthetic injection.'

Lifting the front paw, Joanna held it out for Paul to clip some of the fur away, then when Liz handed him the syringe, she pressed hard to bring up the vein.

'Hold her now with all your strength,' said Paul warningly, and slipped in the needle. Immediately there was a loud, protesting snarl as Chloe tried to pull her paw away and for a tense moment it looked at though the needle would come out, but Joanna held on grimly until suddenly the tiger's head sagged and she went limp.

With the needle still in, Paul waited for a few moments, then gently he opened the tigress's mouth. There was no resistance and then, after testing her good eye for reflex action, he withdrew the needle.

'Right,' he said. 'Now let's get her upside down.'

'May I watch?' asked the keeper, 'or shall I distract you?'

'No—just so long as you don't talk,' said Paul. 'It's really quite a simple operation, but it needs concentration. You see where the lower lid of the eyelid is turned in? That's the cause of the trouble. The eyelids are in direct contact with the eye. It's a condition that sometimes occurs in animals and it's just a question of plastic surgery. I shall take a piece of skin, the shape of a half-moon, from below the eyelid, draw the skin together, pull the eyelid down and stitch on the piece. In about ten days' time Chloe will have a normal eye.' He glanced up at Joanna. 'I expect you've done this op plenty of times—you'll know the most tricky part.'

She nodded, smiling. 'Yes. It's cutting out the skin from below the eyelid. If you take out too much the whole eyelid will be distorted and if you take out too little, it won't pull the eyelid down enough.'

He grinned. 'Exactly. That's why I don't want any distractions.'

In a very short time it was all over, and when Paul stood back surveying his work, the keeper gave a long sigh of relief.

Joanna asked, 'What's the arrangement? Do we keep her here until she's round from the anaesthetic?'

'No. George is going to take her back in his van and as they've got a good recovery cage at the zoo, he'll look after her.' Paul turned to the keeper. 'I'll drop in tomorrow and check to see that everything is OK.' He paused. 'I'll help you out with her. She'll be quite a weight.'

Offered a coffee, the keeper declined with a grin. 'No, thanks. I know she's not due to come round for a few hours, but you never know, and I don't fancy getting stuck in a traffic jam with an indignant tiger!'

'Well, that was a very satisfying job.' Paul came back into the surgery smiling. 'Does it merit a coffee? I could do with one.'

For the next quarter of an hour the atmosphere was relaxed and friendly, and when he had gone and Clare had returned to her office, Liz said,

'Well, I'm off to the stable. It needs a bit of a clean.' She laughed. 'Would you like me to bring Lucky in for a while? That's if I can drag her away from Jenny.'

'Yes, that's a good idea. I hardly ever see her nowadays. Bring her up to my flat. I don't want her to forget her real home. Goodness knows what she'll do when Jenny leaves here.'

When Liz returned with an obviously resentful Lucky the girls watched as she prowled restlessly round the flat, finally jumping on to the windowsill gazing out wistfully. 'It really is going to be a bit of a problem,' said Liz. 'I gather from Paul that, even if the donkey sanctuary is willing to take Jenny, it won't be for a couple of weeks. By that time Lucky will be so attached to her that it will be cruel to separate them.'

Joanna nodded thoughtfully. 'Perhaps the donkey sanctuary would take Lucky as well—what do you think?'

'Would you mind?'

Joanna shrugged. 'Well, not really. She's more devoted to Jenny than she is to me. I'll ask Paul what he thinks.'

That afternoon Chrissie came in half an hour late looking so happy that Joanna stared at her curiously.

'I've just been talking to Mark in the yard and—oh, I don't know—but he seems different somehow. What's more, he says he can manage the cinema this evening after all. I'm absolutely thrilled to bits. Isn't it wonderful?'

Joanna nodded in smiling agreement, and when, a few minutes later, Clare came out of her office the atmosphere was easy with no backbiting from either of them. It really was extraordinary, Joanna reflected a little scornfully, that the two girls should be so worked up by two quite ordinary men. Then, with a quick pang of remembrance, she reproached herself for half despising them. She had been in the same foolish state not so very long ago, but for her it had all ended in tears. Well, never again, she told herself firmly, never again. The last words echoed in her mind for a few minutes until, slowly, she began to question such an unrealistic commitment for the future and re-phrased it. Not for a long time, anyway. It would be very difficult for her to put her trust in any man again.

Dinner with Andrew was pleasant at first, but soon Joanna saw there was going to be the usual problem. He had said he didn't believe in wasting time, and this statement was borne out when he kissed her goodnight outside the surgery.

'I've never believed in love at first sight,' he said quietly, 'but now I'm forced to admit it does happen.'

'No—' she pulled herself out of his arms, 'please don't spoil things, Andrew. It's lovely to be friends, but let's leave it at that for a while. I hardly know you and you certainly don't know me.'

'Enough,' he said thickly, and reached out for her again, but she evaded him. 'Aren't you going to ask me up to your flat for a coffee?' He sounded hurt, but she was firm.

'Only if you promise to keep your distance.'

He nodded reluctantly and followed her upstairs. He remained silent while she put on a kettle and assembled the coffee cups, steadfastly avoiding the pleading look in his eyes. Then suddenly, as she passed the window, she saw a light switch on in the surgery below.

'That's funny,' she stood gazing at the yard, 'I turned off the light at the top of the stairs, didn't I?' She paused. 'I'll have to go and see who's there.'

'I'll come with you.' Andrew got up quickly. 'Can't be too careful. It might be someone breaking in. All those drugs——'

The idea surprised her, but she had to admit he was

right.

'Let me go first,' he said, but his caution was unnecessary, for as they opened the door very quietly, Paul looked up from the examination table. His eyebrows drew together for a moment at the sight of Andrew, then he said abruptly, 'A dog run over on the main road. Hit and run—the car made off. This poor little devil was found in the gutter. Being available I went out to see what I could do.' He paused and passed his hand over the muddy, tangled heap lying ominously still, 'Probably a stray—no collar and thin as a rake.' He stood erect and looked at Joanna and Andrew unsmilingly. 'I'm sorry to disturb you. I can deal with him, so there's no need to stay.'

Andrew came forward, his face alight with interest. 'I'd like to see what you're going to do. What's your diagnosis? He looks a pretty hopeless case to me.'

Paul hesitated, then said slowly, 'I'm inclined to agree. I think the poor blighter has had it. See his gums—he lifted the dog's lips, 'very, very pale. Internal bleeding, I suspect. Otherwise there's not much to see. No bones broken, just badly bruised, but his liver may have been crushed, in which case there's not much hope.' He paused. 'Nevertheless I'll put him on a drip. It might save him.'

'Wouldn't it be better to put him to sleep straight away? If, as you think, he's a stray, there's not much future for him anyway.'

'Is that how you'd treat a human?' Paul glanced up from fixing the equipment. 'You look shocked, and no wonder. But my job as a vet is to save life too.'

Abashed, Andrew made no reply and stood in silence watching the bubbles coming up into the bottle. After a while Paul took out his stethoscope and listened to the dog's heart, then once more he looked at his gums. 'I'll give him another injection, but I don't think there's much hope,' he said quietly.

Joanna turned to Andrew. 'Do you think then that it's ridiculous to spend time, use expensive equipment, in the knowledge that there'll be no payment, no owner to express gratitude—no reason at all in fact for trying to save an insignificant animal?'

He shook his head slowly. 'No, I don't think that now. I have a strange feeling of—how shall I put it?—well, a feeling of humility that vets can be so caring. Not just for the pretty little pets or the useful farm animals but the waifs and strays that come their way. It's opened my eyes considerably.' He paused, then added with a rueful grin, 'And, of course, vets do the whole thing, don't they? Diagnosis, treatment, operations, anaesthesia, dispensing—the lot.'

'Ah, but there's one area in which your responsibility is greater than ours,' Paul said suddenly. 'There's no doubt that a human life is more valuable than that of an animal. Yes, we comfort weeping owners, but I know for certain that I couldn't face up to trying to console a mother whose child is dying. Your triumphs must be greater and your failures more tragic than ours. So don't talk to me about feeling humble!'

Joanna shot a quick glance at Andrew and saw him nod gratefully at Paul's generous tribute to his work, then suddenly her attention was drawn back to the dog on the table. Its breathing was slowing down and, a few minutes later, there was a long pause, one more breath and that was all. Paul heaved a deep sigh as he unfastened the drip and Joanna said quickly,

'Come up and have coffee with us. I'm sure you could do with one.'

He turned to look at her steadily and she found herself unable to read the expression in his eyes. 'I'd rather go home, but thanks all the same.'

Upstairs Andrew sat over his coffee deep in thought for so long that at last Joanna said lightly,

'Penny for them, Andrew.'

He looked up. 'Sorry—I'm not a very good guest, am I?' He paused, frowning slightly. 'I was thinking about you. How long must I keep my distance, as you so firmly put it?'

'No time limit,' Joanna smiled, but her heart sank a little at his persistence. 'Let's just be friends for a bit. I don't want to commit myself to anything just yet.'

Reluctantly he left it at that, and when he had gone, Joanna sat for a while trying to sort out the confusion in her mind. Andrew was attractive—no doubt about that. Kind too, and that was very important. But there was something missing. He lit no spark in her, his kisses meant nothing, and she knew that if she never saw him again it would leave her unmoved. She sighed. Perhaps she would never again experience the passionate love she had felt for James. So passionate that she had only been saved from giving in to his demands by the intervention of a disastrous accident. Disastrous? Was it really? No—not for her.

Suddenly she saw it all from a different angle. If James had not been drowned she would only have found out that he was married when it was too late. The discovery that he was a liar and a cheat would have hurt her much, much more. All the same, it had left a bitterness in her heart, a feeling that no man could be trusted, and that, no doubt, was why she had turned into what Sandy Wilson called an iceberg. To which Paul had added, 'cold and hard'. Was that really true? Would she never fall in love again?

The thought was depressing and, for a moment, her eyes misted over. Then, impatiently, she pulled herself together. Just because she felt nothing for Andrew it did not mean that there would never be anyone else. Meantime she had her work which was, she realised suddenly, even more interesting in this new job than it had been with Mr Bridges. Her colleagues too, although at times exasperating, were broadening her outlook. Paul Copeland, for instance. As a vet she admired him enormously, as a man—well, at times she positively hated him. Those were the times when he was at his most cynical, though lately, having heard his past history, she was beginning to understand that perhaps he was justified in his attitude towards women. Then, of course, the fact that he had family links in Suffolk had made her wary of him right from the start of their acquaintance. But he was, she had to admit, an interesting man. Interesting and—she paused, trying to analyse her feelings—well, yes, he was attractive. Very masculine, proud, rather arrogant, yet underneath the image he presented to the world there was great sensitivity. Staring ahead as she pondered, she found herself gazing at the clock on the wall. Heavens, how late it was! Time for bed and hopefully a dreamless sleep.

But there she was unlucky. Vivid pictures passed before her as she tossed and turned restlessly, and the ones that predominated were those of Paul—one moment goading her into anger, the next moving her to compassionate sympathy with his love and tenderness towards animals. His eyes, sometimes blazing with anger, sometimes serious and gentle, haunted her so much that in her half drowsy state it seemed as though she would never be happy until she had discovered what lay behind that cynical veneer.

In the morning she woke feeling as though she had learnt something of paramount importance and, sipping her breakfast coffee, she tried to sort out the confusion in her mind. At last, recalling the way her brain had revolved around Paul, she smiled wryly at the distorted pictures of semi-consciousness. Crazy fantasies, she told herself scornfully, caused by an evening of mixed impressions. Work, she decided, was the best way to clear her mind, and work she found in plenty when the morning surgery began.

Patient after patient was examined, diagnosed and treated. Owners were as varied as the animals and the

telephone rang incessantly. It was while Joanna was looking
down an auroscope into a dog's ear that Liz turned from the
telephone and held out the receiver. 'A personal call for
Paul—do you happen to know where he is? Clare isn't in her
office.'

Joanna shook her head, then, after explaining the
situation to the caller, Liz said, 'Would you like to leave a
message? Miss Bramford or I will give it to him when he
comes in.' She listened a moment longer, then turned again
to Joanna. 'She'd like to speak to you—it's Paul's sister.'

Joanna put down the auroscope. 'Hold this dog, will you,
please? I've got to look in its ear again. I think there's a grass
seed there.'

Picking up the receiver, she said, 'Can I help you? I'm
Joanna Bramford—the small animal vet.'

A pleasant, friendly voice answered her. 'You don't know
me—I'm Paul Copeland's sister—but I've heard lots about
you. You come from our part of the world, don't you?'

'Yes, I do.' Joanna managed to keep her sudden agitation
under control. 'Would you like me to give a message to
Paul?'

'Just tell him I'd like a chat with him and, if he rings this
evening, I'll be at home.' She paused. 'I'm a client of Mr
Bridges—your old employer. He sends his regards and
hopes you'll look him up when you're down this way again.'

Thanking her, Joanna replaced the receiver, telling herself
that the chill of apprehension she felt was stupid and
unnecessary. Such exaggerated fears really must be
conquered. Mr Bridges was the last person to gossip about
her, so there was no need to worry on that score. But how
had Paul's sister heard 'lots about her'? Going back to the
dog waiting patiently under Liz's soothing care, she picked
up the auroscope—and all at once, the answer to her
question flashed into her mind. Of course. Paul, evidently in
close contact by telephone with his family, had at some time
or other spoken of her to his sister, telling her that the new
small animal vet had worked with Mr Bridges. Suddenly

aware that Liz was staring at her, she resumed her examination of the dog's ear.

At last she said, 'There's a grass seed there all right, rather deeply embedded. I'll try to get it out with forceps, so hold him as tightly as you can. I don't want to hurt him.'

But the dog began to get hysterical and resignedly Joanna gave up the struggle. 'It means a full anaesthetic,' she said. 'Will you ask his owner to come in, please?'

Asked if the dog had had a meal, his mistress said ruefully, 'Not a thing. All he's done is to shake his head and whine. Kept me awake most of the night.'

'Well, in that case, I'll do it directly after surgery,' said Joanna. 'You can fetch him this evening.'

With two female cats to spay, one tom to neuter and now the grass seed patient, there was no time for a coffee break, especially as Clare was still absent.

'Where on earth has she got to?' asked Liz, exasperated at having to pass on calls from farms to the vets concerned. 'She might at least have rung to tell us she was taking the morning off.'

'Well, I forgot. Anyhow, I'm here now.' Clare appeared suddenly in the doorway, her hands full of shopping bags. 'I've been shopping—new clothes. I had to get some—haven't a thing to wear.'

'Well, neither have I come to that,' Liz said sharply. 'Surely it wasn't all that urgent. I should have thought——' With a quick cautionary glance at Liz Joanna stopped the threatened quarrel and, unusually, Clare did not take offence.

'I've got some lovely things,' she said jubilantly. 'There's a new shop in the High Street and I just had to have a look around and ended up buying some things that Freddy will adore. He says he likes bright colours, and these are out of this world!'

Going into the office, she shut the door firmly behind her.

Half to herself Joanna murmured, 'She's terribly insecure. Let's hope she's at last found what she's subconsciously seeking.'

Liz looked up in surprise. 'What makes you so knowledgeable about people, Joanna?'

'Knowledgeable? Me——' Joanna pondered for a moment, then shook her head. 'No, it's not that. It's only my intuition—call it what you will.'

'Oh, I think intuition is the right word,' Paul's deep voice came from behind Joanna as he stood in the doorway, causing her to flush deeply with embarrassment.

He came forward, his eyes full of mockery. 'That's the thing that women pride themselves on, though from what I hear it very often lets them down. It's a poor substitute for level-headed judgement.'

Joanna's smile faded. Was it just her imagination or was he hinting at some hidden knowledge of her past? Suddenly she remembered his sister's telephone message and, watching his face carefully, she passed it on to him, adding, 'Your sister—I don't know her married name—said she'd be at home this evening.'

'Thank you. Her name is Tessa Rogers.' He paused. 'How did you know she was married?'

'Well, I haven't been able to recall anyone of the name of Copeland in Mr Bridges' files——' Joanna stopped. Oh dear! What a giveaway! Paul would now realise that she had been giving the matter a great deal of thought. Still watching him warily, she saw no indication that the idea had occurred to him and sighed with relief. Then just as she was relaxing he said,

'Tessa says Mr Bridges is missing you badly. His present assistant is not satisfactory. Apparently he very much regrets that you didn't take up his offer of a partnership. I must say that makes me quite curious. I would have jumped at it in your place. A nice little practice in the heart of Suffolk. Why on earth——'?' He broke off abruptly at the sight of her face from which Joanna herself could feel the colour receding.

For a moment she could find no answer, then, pulling herself together, she said coolly, 'Well, I gather you were offered a partnership here which you declined. But that's your affair, isn't it?'

'Oh dear! Snubbed again!' Paul's mouth twitched humorously, then seeing that Liz was looking puzzled at the exchange between the two vets, he said, 'By the way, I've increased Jenny's diet a little. I've put the new directions up on the wall, so stick to them rigorously, will you, please?' He turned away and opened the office door. 'Clare, I'll pick you up at eleven o'clock on Saturday. That's if you still want to go to the donkey sanctuary.'

'Oh, yes. I'll be ready.' Clare said eagerly, then added, 'Would you like me to bring a packed lunch?'

'No, thanks. We'll have something at a pub. See you then.'

As the outer door closed behind him Liz said softly, 'I'm surprised that Clare is still interested in going. I would have thought an outing with Paul would have faded into insignificance compared with the arrival of the new vet. Mrs Holman told me that he's coming on Saturday afternoon.' She shrugged. 'Still, perhaps she thinks it's best to have two strings to her bow. Or rather—' she burst out laughing, 'two beaux to her string!'

'What's the joke?' Clare came out of the office and Joanna, seeing the guilty look on the other girl's face, said quickly, 'Oh, Clare, I like that skirt. Was that one of the things you bought this morning?'

'Yes.' Clare turned round for their inspection. 'It's nice, isn't it? Shall I show you the rest?'

'Good idea. You and Liz can have a fashion show. I can't come in just yet—I've got some work to do here.'

Nothing loath, the girls went into the office and, listening to Liz's admiring remarks and Clare's excited explanations, Joanna felt a glow of satisfaction. This was the atmosphere she wanted in the surgery. Liz, of course, was fairly easygoing, but Chrissie might be more difficult. Still, if she and Mark became close then presumably she would be more tolerant of Clare's moods. In any case, Clare would eventually return to her original office—repairs were now progressing well—then life would be even more pleasant. Of course there was no denying that Clare would always be touchy and quick to take offence, and if the new vet did not come up to her expectations then there would be trouble ahead for everyone.

Joanna sighed. Her own affairs were not going to be as easy to sort out. She was going to have to tread very warily with regard to Andrew Porter. With only a little encouragement from her the friendship between them would rapidly become too serious for her liking.

A sudden burst of laughter from the office caused her spirits to rise and she smiled involuntarily. No need to get too apprehensive. She wanted a better social life, and Andrew was a good beginning.

Half an hour later, having viewed and praised various outfits shown by Clare, Joanna said, 'I'm just going down to the sta le to have a look at Lucky. Her stitches are due out soon and I want to make sure she hasn't pulled any of them out.'

Liz laughed. 'Poor Joanna! Lucky has quite deserted you—does she come in at night?'

'No.' Joanna smiled ruefully. 'She sometimes roams round the yard, but she always returns to Jenny and snuggles down beside her. She purrs affectionately when I put food down for her, but that's the extent of her interest in me. Still, it's worth it just to see how Jenny enjoys her company.'

Jenny had other company as well when Joanna arrived at the stable. Mrs Holman said, 'I come down most days, you know. Poor Jenny, she's so pathetically grateful.' She stroked the donkey's soft nose. 'Paul is doing so much for her—let's hope she'll recover sufficiently to enjoy life.' She watched while Lucky was being examined. 'Is she OK?'

Joanna nodded. 'Yes. The stitches are all intact. I'd take

it personally if they weren't.' She laughed as Lucky jumped out of her arms and walked solemnly round Jenny's foot purring loudly.

Mrs Holman smiled and fondled the donkey's ears. 'I think we're superfluous here. Come and have a coffee with me—that's if you've got time.'

'Well, it's a bit late,' Joanna glanced at her watch, 'but all the same I should love one. I'll just pop in and tell Clare and Liz where to find me.'

A few minutes later as she sat opposite Mrs Holman the conversation came round to the Mayfields' party.

'I thought you looked absolutely beautiful,' Mrs Holman said. 'That lovely dress and your hair round your shoulders—stunning, as I heard Dr Porter say to himself when he first saw you. You made an immediate hit there. How did you enjoy yesterday evening with him?' She laughed. 'Don't look so surprised! Of course I guessed who you were with when you left the hotel telephone number in case of emergency. As a matter of fact there was one—an emergency, I mean—a dog that Paul went out to and brought back to the surgery. It died, didn't it?'

'Yes.' Joanna frowned. 'I suppose that call should really have been put through to me. Why did Paul take on the case?'

'He said it would be a pity to break up your evening out and as he was available——' Mrs Holman paused. 'I thought it was rather kind of him.'

'Yes, of course. But how did he get the call?'

'Oh, he was here with us when the call came in. He'd been down the yard with Jenny and my husband asked him in for a drink. He—Paul—seemed very depressed about something. It wasn't Jenny—she's going on quite well——' Mrs Holman shrugged. 'Well, you know me, curious to a degree, so I tried to find out what was wrong, but he didn't open up. Poor Paul, I do wish he could find a girl he could love and be loved in return.'

Joanna looked doubtful. 'I don't think that's his trouble.

It seems to me that he goes out of his way to antagonise women. It's as though—' she stopped. She must watch what she said. Kind as Mrs Holman was, it might be dangerous to show any interest that could be interpreted wrongly. Rather lamely she added, 'Actually I haven't given much thought to Paul. He and I don't get on too well, you know.'

'That's what surprises me.' Mrs Holman gazed at Joanna searchingly. 'When you arrived here my first reaction was—just the girl for Paul.'

'What?' Genuine amazement showed in Joanna's face. 'Oh, surely not! In any case——'

'In any case you've now got someone else,' the other woman nodded, 'Andrew Porter. Now that looks promising to me.'

'Oh, dear!' Joanna felt a spurt of irritation but managed to cover it up by laughing. 'Mrs Holman, you're a terrible matchmaker! Andrew Porter is nice enough and it's pleasant to be taken out. That's all, I assure you.' She paused. 'I was wondering how to get some kind of social life away from the practice, as I think I told you, and Andrew—' she shrugged, 'well, he's not bad to start with.'

'Heartless girl!' Mrs Holman shook her head in mock reproach. 'All the same, I don't blame you. There's safety in numbers. Which reminds me—will you be coming in on Saturday or is it your weekend off?'

'No, that's next weekend. Why?'

'Well, Freddy Conway—the new vet—is arriving then. About the middle of the afternoon, I think, so I'll give him tea. Come along and join us, will you? I wanted Clare to come as well, but she's off to the donkey sanctuary with Paul.' She gave a puzzled frown. 'You know, that surprises me too. She was so keen on Freddy at the party and I should have thought she would have made it her business to welcome him. Still, perhaps she also thinks there's safety in numbers.' She laughed. 'You girls! I find it most intriguing.'

Intriguing was the word, Joanna thought as she made her

way back to the surgery. Clare must obviously regret not being able to welcome Freddy, but with her need to confess all to Paul she clearly had no option.

That evening, after a tiring surgery, Joanna was luxuriating in a relaxing bath when she heard the telephone ringing in the other room. Hastily wrapping herself in a large bath towel, she went to pick up the receiver.

'Joanna—' Andrew's voice was eager, 'I'm off duty on Saturday. Can you manage to get the day off and come out with me? Somewhere in the country or down to the coast—whatever you like. Say yes, please. It seems ages since I last saw you.'

Joanna frowned ruefully. 'I'm so sorry, Andrew. It's not my weekend off. Another time, perhaps.' She paused and added a little mockingly, 'It isn't all that long either. Two days, in fact.'

'Two long days. What are you doing now?'

She told him, but before he could suggest coming round to see her she added quickly, 'After that I'm going to bed early. I've had a hard day and I'm tired.'

Regretfully he gave in, but not without making her promise that she would go out with him as soon as they could make their days off coincide. Returning to her bath, she relaxed once more. It was strange, she reflected idly, that Andrew Porter, attractive, amusing and obviously very interested in her, aroused no strong feelings beyond those of friendship. Perhaps, as she grew to know him better, she might become more fond of him, but that would be all. Maybe she should make that clear to him as soon as possible, otherwise he might get hurt. It was unfair to lead him on—to allow him to hope—he was too nice a man to treat in such a cold-hearted way. Having made her decision she found it was comparatively easy to put him out of her head. Was that, she wondered, suddenly depressed, how it was going to be in future? Would no man ever take James' place? There seemed to be no answer to that question, though it haunted her for the rest of the evening. Her sleep was troubled and confused, for once again she dreamt of Paul Copeland. One moment he seemed arrogant and overbearing, filling her subconscious mind with uneasiness, the next, compassionate and tender, causing her to suspect guiltily that she had misjudged him.

She woke next morning feeling disturbed. Paul Copeland was the last man she wanted to dream about. Still, perhaps it was a sign that the painful memories of the past were fading and that her new job and her colleagues were now absorbing all her thoughts.

CHAPTER SIX

LIZ and Chrissie took alternative Saturdays off, but Chrissie was late that morning and Joanna was forced to begin surgery without her. The first patient was a young but very large German Shepherd dog. To Joanna's dismay it was completely uncontrollable and the owner—a girl of about fourteen—was quite unable to hold the dog still. Impatiently Joanna looked out of the window in the hope of seeing Chrissie at last, but the only person visible was a man striding up the yard. As he drew near she recognised Paul and, impulsively, she opened the window and called to him. The huge dog was roaming round the room when he came in and Joanna quickly explained the situation.

He nodded calmly, took a tape from his pocket, and approached the dog quietly. Seizing his opportunity, he suddenly whipped the noose round the dog's nose and tied it firmly.

'Now for an exhibition of masculine strength,' he said drily, and lifted the struggling animal on to the table, holding him in an iron grip. The job of clipping the dog's nails was soon done and Joanna sighed with relief as the owner was tugged away by her unmanageable pet.

'Thank you, Paul,' she smiled at him gratefully, 'you got me out of a very awkward predicament. How lucky that you were in the yard.'

'I was just having a look at Jenny before I go to the donkey sanctuary. It's amazing how much work the farrier has been able to do. I'm hoping the sanctuary will take her in soon. I can't keep her much longer in the yard stable—one never knows when it may be needed.'

'Will there be a vet attending the sanctuary?'

'Yes, and that's a bit of luck, because I know him. We qualified together and if they take Jenny down there I know she'll be in good hands. I'll go and visit her, of course.' He paused. 'Would you like to come with me if and when we transport her there?' Paul hesitated. 'Oh, I know you refused to go out with me socially, but this would be different. A mutual professional interest. I think you'd find the sanctuary interesting.'

Joanna drew a long breath. Why not? she asked herself. It was high time to call a truce—to refuse would be churlish. She nodded. 'I'd like that, but it might be rather difficult to arrange. Time off, and all that.'

'Oh, we could work it somehow. With this new man and Mark and Mr Holman around there'd be someone to help out with emergencies. In any case I think it would be best to make it a Sunday—no regular surgeries for you.' Suddenly Paul frowned. 'But perhaps your Sundays will be taken up in future.'

'How do you mean?'

'Well—' Paul's mouth twisted sardonically, 'your new love—Andrew Porter. He'll be wanting all your spare time.'

Joanna's face clouded for a moment, then, remembering her resolution to laugh at his snide remarks, she said scornfully, 'why does it always have to be "love"? Andrew is a friend, that's all.'

His eyes swept over her and he laughed grimly. 'No man could possibly be content with a platonic friendship with a girl as beautiful as you. If you think overwise then either you don't realise how desirable you are or you just don't understand men.' He stopped, seeing the flame of anger in her eyes, then he added quietly, 'No need to fly off the handle. It's true. You are utterly—' suddenly he took her in his arms, crushing her against him—'irresistible.' His mouth stopped her furious gasp and then her head swam under the passion of his kiss. It was all so unexpected that she was trembling with shock when at last he released her, and staring at him accusingly she saw that his face was pale and drawn and his hands were clenched tightly at his sides. There was a long silence, then, shaking his head as though bewildered, he turned, the door slammed and he was gone.

In spite of the sound of barking coming from the waiting room Joanna remained still, unable to bring herself back to reality. So that was all that men saw in her! A desirable sex object—no more, no less. A surge of furious resentment rose in her as she pulled herself together. James must have looked on her in the same way and Andrew—well, he spoke of love at first sight, but that was only another name for physical attraction. There was, however, one difference. Andrew's kisses left her unmoved, whereas Paul—no, she would not allow herself to dwell on that shattering experience. And the way in which he had slammed out of the room indicated that he too would prefer to forget his momentary lack of self-control. She must forget it herself and treat the whole episode lightly. She pushed back her hair, tumbling about her face after Paul's rough onslaught, and went towards the waiting room, glancing out of the window as she passed. Oh, thank goodness, there was Chrissie at last.

She came in, flustered and apologetic. 'I'm terribly sorry. I forgot to set my alarm and I slept on and on. Last night——'

'Don't bother now,' Joanna said sharply. 'Clients are getting impatient—we can't waste any more time.'

Luckily most of the cases were routine, but towards the end of surgery a cat was brought in by a middle-aged lady who said breathlessly, 'He's choking and retching. Do you think there's something stuck in his throat?'

Lifting the cat out of its basket, Joanna searched for the cause of the trouble. Crouching on the table, dribbling heavily with long strands of saliva hanging from its mouth, the cat was very distressed. His back arched, he was making horrible croaking sounds, stretching out his head and occasionally clawing at his throat. His mistress said, 'I've managed to look at his mouth, but I can't see anything. I suppose it could be a bone stuck further down, but I never give him bones, so what on earth is wrong?'

With Chrissie holding the cat firmly it suddenly became pathetically docile, as though sensing that help was at hand, and opening the wet salivary mouth wide Joanna examined the interior. She was about to shake her head when, suddenly, her attention was arrested. 'I can see something—it looks like a bit of cotton. Right at the back of the throat.' She stood silent for a moment, pondering, then she looked up at the cat's mistress. 'I daren't pull it because it might be attached to—well, anything. A necklace—a needle——'

'A needle! Oh, goodness! It might be that,' the owner gasped in dismay. 'I'm a dressmaker and Timmy was with me this morning in my workroom.' Her eyes filled with frightened tears. 'Will it kill him if he's swallowed it?'

'I can't be sure it is a needle,' Joanna spoke carefully, 'though it certainly sounds the most likely thing. It depends where it's lodged. In order to find out I shall have to anaesthetise him. Has he eaten today?'

'Goodness, no—he was far too upset. Can you do it now?'

'Yes, immediately. It can't be left.' Joanna turned to Chrissie. 'Will you look in the waiting room, please, and explain the situation?'

A minute later Chrissie returned. 'Only one dog, nothing urgent. They said they'd come back on Monday.'

As soon as the door closed Chrissie filled a syringe, put it on the table, and Joanna clipped short the hair on the front of the cat's forepaw. After cleansing the skin with antiseptic she picked up the syringe and waited while Chrissie gripped the paw below the elbow and brought up the vein. As Joanna pushed in the needle and Chrissie released the pressure Timmy tried frantically to jerk back, but, held firmly, he could not move and the needle remained in place. Within seconds the cat relaxed and, after a pause, Joanna injected a little more anaesthetic. Watching her patient carefully, she tested his reactions, then eased his tongue out so that it hung from the side of his mouth. Another shot of anaesthetic and she stood back, withdrawing the syringe.

Chrissie asked, 'Why did you do it that way? I thought you would have injected it into the chest.'

'He'll come round quickly with the short-acting anaesthetic,' Joanna said, and began looking down the throat with an auroscope. 'Ah, here it is. Yes—the head of a needle embedded in the back of—right back—almost too far. May I have the forceps, please?'

Slowly and carefully she drew the needle out, along with several more inches of cotton, and both girls sighed with relief.

'He'll come round fairly soon,' said Joanna, 'but he'll be a bit dopey, so he'd better stay here for a few hours.'

His joyful owner said she would go and do her Saturday shopping and added remorsefully, 'I'll be very careful in future. In fact, I won't let him in my workroom ever again.'

When she had gone Chrissie said reflectively, 'The amazing things that can happen to animals. To humans too, come to that.' She paused, her face lighting up. 'Oh, Joanna—last night with Mark! It was the most wonderful evening of my life.'

Joanna smiled. 'What happened? Tell me all—you know you're dying to.'

'Well, we had a meal first, then we went to see the film. After that we drove down to the coast and sat in the car, looking at the sea. We kissed and talked and we talked and kissed. No more than that—Mark isn't the type to—well, you know what I mean. But it was all so wonderful that I still feel up in the clouds. We're going out again tomorrow evening and I really think—' she stopped as the telephone rang. 'Oh, dear! I must come down to earth.'

A moment later she held out the receiver. 'It's Mrs Langton. She lives about two miles from here, past the Mayfields' house. Her old dog has had a bad heart attack and she's afraid to move him. Could you go along as soon as possible?'

'I'll go now.' Joanna picked up her case. 'Let's see—respiratory stimulant, syringe—tablets—yes, all in order. See you later.'

She was approaching the Mayfields' house when she saw a car coming down the drive, and as it waited before turning into the main road she recognised it at once. Glancing at the clock on her dashboard, she noted that it was half past eleven and smiled a little wryly. Half an hour later in leaving—probably Clare's fault and, judging from the expression on Paul's face, he was not in the best of tempers. She waved as she went past and Paul flashed his headlights in response, but Clare made no acknowledgment. With an unaccountable pang in her heart Joanna tried to analyse her feelings. Why on earth did she feel so envious of Clare? A pretty girl sitting beside Paul and going on a pleasurable trip with him—well, it was stupid to want to change places with her. And if Clare carried out her intention to unburden her conscience the trip would be far from pleasant. Hastily she pushed aside her slight feeling of desolation, and as she pulled up outside the house she was seeking she saw a lady standing at the open door.

Mrs Langton's eyes were red with weeping as she led Joanna into her kitchen and pointed to a little Yorkshire terrier lying on a rug. 'Bobby is very old—fourteen—and nearly blind. When Miss Russell came out to see him last she said he might go at any time. She gave me some tablets for him and I ought to have got some more, but he seemed better and I forgot.'

Joanna nodded and went down on her knees beside her patient. His breathing was laboured and he seemed now to be in a coma. A few minutes later she rose to her feet and took off her stethoscope. Opening her case, she took out a syringe, but before filling it with a heart and respiratory stimulant she turned to Mrs Langton.

'I'm sorry,' she said compassionately, 'but, in view of his age, the chances of saving him are fairly remote. He'll probably come round again with an injection, but he really hasn't much longer to live. His heart is—well, worn out. Don't you think—' she paused, then added carefully, 'wouldn't it be better to put him to sleep now and save him any further suffering?'

'Oh no! I couldn't possibly——' Mrs Langton wrung her hands. 'I'll look after him properly. Just tell me what to do.'

Joanna sighed. 'Well, this injection—' she filled the syringe, slipped in the needle and massaged the area to help the disposal of the drug '—and these tablets may keep him going a little longer. Make sure you don't run out of them and make sure you don't get too upset yourself or the dog will feel your distress.' She sighed again. 'That's all I can do, I'm afraid.'

Some time later, back in the surgery, Joanna answered the telephone. 'Bobby has gone,' Mrs Langton sobbed. 'He's just had another attack—it was very severe and he died in a few minutes. I'm heartbroken. It was so sad.'

Sad for the little dog too, Joanna said to herself as she replaced the receiver. He could have been spared that if only—she gave herself a mental shake. It was always terribly difficult for people to make the final decision even when there was obviously no hope. Her depression was lifted at the sound of Chrissie humming to herself in the dispensary. Smiling, she recalled how astonished Mark had been when told of Chrissie's interest in him. It was pleasing to know that the information he had been given had had the desired effect. Strange how one thing led to another. If Chrissie had not overslept there would have been no need to call Paul in to help with the German Shepherd dog and the resultant scene with him would never have happened.

Even now, the memory of his passionate kiss made her heart beat too fast for comfort, and she realised that anger was not the predominant emotion she was feeling. Gazing unseeingly out of the window, she shivered suddenly as a blinding revelation stared her in the face. No—she shook her head violently—no, that was impossible. One kiss, forced on her against her will—that was no prelude to falling in love. It proved merely that she, in her turn, found Paul physically attractive. What of it? she asked herself defiantly; what if the remembrance of his strength, those hard, muscular arms holding her helpless, filled her with a yearning for more—it simply meant that his masculinity had stirred her out of the apathy in which she had been enveloped for so long. It meant only that she was not the iceberg Sandy had dubbed her. One day she might fall in love again, but with a man who would love her in return. Smiling a little bitterly, she reflected that, in a way, she owed Paul a debt of gratitude for having cleared her mind, but she must take care that it didn't happen again.

The telephone brought her back to earth and thankfully she heard Mrs Holman's voice.

'Freddy Conway has just rung to say he'll be arriving about three-thirty. I'll expect you then. Is that OK?'

Joanna glanced at her watch and explained the situation to Chrissie. 'I'll hold the fort,' she promised, and added mischievously, 'I'll bet this Freddy will fall for you. Clare will be furious, of course.'

'Don't be silly!' Joanna said sharply. 'Why must you look on me as a kind of——'

'Femme fatale?' Chrissie giggled, then seeing Joanna's frown she subsided. 'OK, I'm sorry. But you don't realise the effect you have on men, do you?' She paused. 'I expect that's why Clare has gone out with Paul. She sees that he's very interested in you and even though she likes Freddy Conway she still wants to keep tabs on Paul. That's what Liz says, anyhow.'

'The gossip that goes on in this practice is unbelievable, and what's more, it's totally inaccurate,' said Joanna scornfully, then seeing Chrissie flush at the rebuke she added more kindly, 'I don't mean to bite your head off, but please stop saying such ridiculous things.'

Chrissie nodded penitently, then, eyes soft and dreamlike, she said, 'I expect it's because of Mark. I'm so much in love that I want everybody else to be happy.'

'A very usual reaction,' Joanna said drily, 'but, as it happens, I'm fancy free and intend to remain that way. I'm also very hungry. Would you like to come and have lunch with me?'

'No, thanks. I'd like to, but I'm meeting Mark at a pub near here—that's if he can get through his calls in time. I'll put the telephone through to your flat for now and later on it can be transferred to Mrs Holman. Will that be all right?'

At half past three there was no sign of Freddy Conway, and Joanna and Mrs Holman sat talking over various cases that had occurred in the practice.

'I've always taken an interest in veterinary work,' Mrs Holman said reminiscently. 'Before we came here Mike ran a branch practice for a vet in the West Country. I used to help in the surgery when the nurse was off duty. But we left after a few years because the practice was getting too big altogether. This one is just right. Mind you, Mr Mayfield is talking of expanding—it's happening everywhere, so I suppose we'll have to go along with it. It's difficult, of course, when you're a partner.' She paused. 'How would you feel about a partnership in a year or so?'

'Goodness!' Joanna's eyes widened. 'I've never got as

far as thinking about such a thing.'

Mrs Holman shrugged. 'Well, it's possible that you'll be asked. Anyway——' She broke off at the sound of the doorbell. 'This must be Freddy Conway.'

It did not take long for Joanna to decide that the new vet was going to be an asset to the practice. Intelligent and talkative with a strong sense of humour, he was full of amusing anecdotes. After a while he began asking questions about his new colleagues and then, quite casually, Clare's name came up in the conversation. 'What exactly,' he asked, 'does she do in the practice?'

For a moment Mrs Holman hesitated and Joanna, remembering how on her first day she had been warned against Clare, hoped fervently that Mrs Holman would be more discreet this time. To her great relief no reference was made as to Clare's difficult character and Freddy Conway said, 'She's a nice girl, isn't she? Very pretty, too.' He grinned. 'I can see I'm going to enjoy being here!'

Later, when Mrs Holman had gone with Freddy to show him the flat he had been allocated, Joanna took Lucky's evening meal down the yard, and as she stood stroking Jenny her thoughts turned inevitably to Paul and Clare. It was to be hoped that Clare would not, after all, attempt to rake up the past. No good could possibly come out of it.

She sighed, and then as she turned away from the stable she saw Paul himself coming down the yard. At the sight of him a sudden, glorious mixture of joy and fear filled her whole being—a revelation of love such as she had never before experienced—and for a minute she stood in a kind of ecstasy. Then as he drew near she saw fury in his face and stiffened in alarm. His dark brows were drawn together in a black frown and in a harsh, almost unrecognisable voice, he said,

'I was looking for you. I'd like an explanation.'

Her eyes widened in shock. 'What—what on earth do

you mean?'

His mouth hardened. 'Don't play the innocent! You know very well what I mean.'

'Of course I don't.' Utterly confused, she stared at him in consternation until at last he said grimly, 'Clare enlivened our journey back from the sanctuary with a tale that would have been better left untold. That in itself was bad enough, but when she added that it was you who had prevailed on her to make this confession I could scarcely believe that anyone could be so cruel.' He paused as he saw her go pale with dismay. 'Yes, I can see that you didn't want me to know that you were behind it. Clare asked me not to tell you that you'd pressurised her into it, but I wouldn't agree to that.' He stopped as Joanna opened her mouth, but in spite of her efforts to speak, no words came. Her throat was dry, her mouth quivered and she could only shake her head in shocked denial. Paul's voice grated as he went on, 'I know—have known from the start, that you dislike me, but to take such a revenge for one impulsive kiss—my God! It's unbelievable!'

'I didn't——' At last Joanna managed to speak. 'Paul—I tried to dissuade her. I knew you'd be hurt. Clare is lying—lying through her teeth. You must take my word for it.'

'Oh, that's great!' The scorn in his voice was terrible to hear. 'Why should she lie when she was confessing her former lies? Why, having kept it dark for so long, should she suddenly have the urge to blurt it all out now?' He took her by the shoulder and shook her. 'It was your influence, wasn't it? Your insidious influence on a stupid girl who foolishly confided in you.' He let her go and stood staring at her contemptuously, his eyes like granite, then he said slowly and deliberately, 'Well, your carefully thought out scheme failed. Clare's confession left me cold. It's all water under the bridge as far as I'm concerned. But it exposed you as a cold-hearted, venomous—' he paused, then gave a short mirthless laugh—'well, thank

God I found out in time.' He turned on his heel, leaving Joanna fighting wildly against the wave of nausea that was sweeping over her.

She shut her eyes and leant against the wall until at last the sickness passed, to be replaced by burning anger. She would never forgive him. Never. Even if Clare eventually owned up; even if Paul went on his knees to apologise, she would never pardon his harsh, unquestioning condemnation.

Suddenly there was a rustling in the straw at her feet and a moment later Lucky jumped up on to her shoulder. A soft velvety paw touched her face, and the unexpected demonstration of affection was all that was needed to release the bitter tears welling up inside her. For a few minutes, with Lucky clasped in her arms, she wept uncontrollably. Then, as Jenny nosed her gently, she thought desolately, animals—they're my real friends. Loving, comforting friends. The only ones you can trust. After a while she wiped her eyes and looked cautiously up the yard. No one must see her tear-stained face. Thankfully she saw that it was all clear and with a quick kiss on Lucky's soft fur and a gentle stroke of Jenny's nose, she fled up to her flat. Eventually, after splashing her eyes with cold water and putting on fresh make-up, she went down to deal with the evening surgery. Clare, she knew, would not be there, but on Monday morning she would confront her and somehow or other force her to admit to her cowardly, deceitful behaviour.

It was when she returned to her flat that the pain of Paul's unjust condemnation returned in full force, and with it came an urgent question. How could she love a man who was so hostile towards her? So harsh in his judgement and so bitter that he would not listen when she had denied his accusation? She must have been fantasising—hopelessly seeking a love that would heal the wound she had suffered in the past. Just because Paul was so different from James she had deluded herself into

thinking that here was a man she could trust never to lie
or deceive her in any way. Well, she would cut that foolish
illusion out of her heart, but one thing was certain. Paul
must learn the truth and then, when Clare had been
exposed, she would put him right out of her mind.

Her resolution made, she tried to distract herself by
cleaning and tidying her flat, and had nearly finished
when the telephone rang. Andrew's voice came as a
complete surprise. She had almost forgotten he existed.

'I'm off duty tomorrow. Do you think you could
manage a few hours with me—the whole day,
preferably?'

Joanna drew a long breath. This was what she needed.
Someone to help her get things in perspective. But a
whole day—that would be difficult. Sandy Wilson had
already left and Freddy was not due to begin work till
Monday. After a few moments' thought she rang through
to Mrs Holman, who said cheerfully, 'Don't worry. We'll
find someone to deal with emergencies. Go out and enjoy
yourself.'

A perfect autumn day with a brilliant blue sky and only
a hint of a nip in the air provided the background to a
long walk after lunch in a pleasant hotel. It should have
dispelled Joanna's melancholy, but, in spite of her efforts,
she was unable to hide her unhappiness from Andrew. At
last, as they were wandering hand in hand through a
beech wood, he pointed to a log lying among the leaves
that covered the ground like a golden carpet.

'Let's sit down for a few minutes,' he said quietly,
'then you can tell me what's troubling you. No, don't
shake your head—I know you're upset about something.'

Glancing at him as she sat down, she saw such
compassionate concern in his eyes that slowly she began to
unburden herself. Andrew's friendly face grew grim as he
listened and slipping a comforting arm round her
shoulders he said, 'What a tangled web of deceit! You're
absolutely right, of course. Somehow or other Clare must

be made to tell Paul the truth. It won't be easy—the girl is a pathological liar.' He paused, his eyes searching Joanna's face, then he added slowly and sadly, 'One thing is horribly plain to me. You're in love with Paul.' He sighed. 'I suppose I should have guessed it from the start—the sharp antagonism that exists between you which so often conceals a smouldering awareness of each other——' He drew a long breath. 'I can see that my own cause is lost.'

'Don't be ridiculous!' Joanna jumped to her feet and stood looking down at him angrily. 'What a crazy diagnosis! I hate Paul—really hate him for the way he's treated me.'

Andrew shook his head, smiling half pityingly in a way that infuriated her still further. 'Hatred is often akin to love.'

'Oh, rubbish! Don't be so smug! You'll be saying next that Paul is in love with me.' Suddenly she relented as she saw the sadness in his eyes and impulsively she added, 'You mustn't jump to conclusions like that. I like you much better than I like Paul. He's been horrible to me, whereas you're kind and compassionate. So kind that I've confided in you, though now I rather wish I hadn't,' she added regretfully.

'I'm glad you did,' he said quietly. 'I know now where I stand.'

Helplessly Joanna gazed at him, then suddenly she bent down and kissed him gently. 'Please, Andrew, don't look so hurt. There's no need. I like you very much. Perhaps——'

'No,' he stood up quickly, 'don't make rash promises, Joanna. Let's settle for friendship.' Then taking her into his arms he kissed her so tenderly that tears of regret filled her eyes.

'Well, now I know for sure.' He let her go and smiled ruefully. 'You pity me, but I've no intention of trading on that.' He laughed self-mockingly. 'My heart isn't broken, I assure you. I've no doubt I shall recover, so cheer up. Let's enjoy the rest of our day together.'

He drove her back to her flat, and she felt drained of all emotion as she watched his car receding into the distance. Her one desire was to sleep and gather strength in which to meet the next day. A day in which she must force Clare to admit her treacherous stab in the back—a difficult task but one in which she simply must succeed. Suddenly to her dismay she heard the insistent ring of the telephone, and her heart sank. An emergency—that was all she needed! She wouldn't get much sleep tonight. Then, astonished, she heard Mrs Holman's voice.

'I know it's late, but I couldn't get you before. Joanna, something awful has happened. Clare has had an accident. She was out riding, and in a narrow lane an impatient motorist rushed past her, causing her horse to shy. She was thrown off and is now in hospital with concussion and a broken leg. Into the bargain her dog Rufus is missing—he was running beside her at the time.' Mrs Holman paused for breath. 'Mrs Mayfield rang to tell us after having been to the hospital. She says Clare is semi-conscious and keeps calling for Rufus, so they're just praying he'll be found before she comes round properly. Freddy Conway and Paul have been very helpful—out for hours trying to find the dog—and the police have been informed. Apparently the driver of the car never stopped and Clare was only found by another motorist.'

Joanna's mind was in a whirl when at last she put down the receiver. Concern for Clare was her first reaction, then, as the news sank in, she realised that her own plans would have to be temporarily abandoned. The thought of enduring Paul's contempt for an indefinite period was unbearable. Should she approach him and try once more to make him believe her explanation? The prospect was daunting and she felt sick at the thought of another failure. An almost sleepless night brought no solution to her problem. All she could hope for was that Paul himself, when he was calmer, might come to doubt the veracity of Clare's story, but that, she felt despairingly, was extremely unlikely.

CHAPTER SEVEN

IMMEDIATELY after morning surgery Joanna went over to see Mrs Holman. 'I've been trying to get Mrs Mayfield,' she explained, 'but the telephone seems to be constantly engaged. Have you any more news of Clare?'

Mrs Holman placed a steaming cup of coffee on the table. 'Drink that. You look tired.' She took a sip from her own cup. 'Well, the latest news is that Clare has recovered consciousness and, all being well, she'll be home towards the end of the week. Her leg will be in plaster, of course, and she won't be coming back to work for some time. In fact I gather from what her mother hinted that she won't be working here any more. Her parents think she ought to be doing something else, something she's more fitted for—working perhaps with animals but not in a veterinary surgery. By the way, I'm going up to see her this afternoon. 'Would you like to come?'

Joanna shook her head. 'I don't think I can manage it. I've got a couple of outside calls to do.' Feeling guilty at the lie, she added hastily, 'Give her my love,' and then felt even more guilty at such hypocrisy. Love was the last thing she felt for Clare.

Mrs Holman passed over the biscuits and said easily, 'Well, in any case, she'll soon be home and then you can go and visit her there. I'm sure she'd like to see you. We've all noticed how much she has improved since you arrived here.'

'I don't think I've made any difference to her,' Joanna said drily, then to hide her bitterness she asked quickly, 'And Rufus—what about him?'

Mrs Holman's pleasant face clouded. 'No luck, so far. The Mayfields hope he'll eventually make his way home—that is, if he hasn't met with an accident. They haven't told Clare yet.' She got up to refill Joanna's cup, then suddenly she pointed to the window. 'There's Paul's car going down the yard and—oh, that's marvellous! See—he's got Rufus.'

As the car went through the open gates and disappeared behind the wall, Mrs Holman said joyfully, 'Let's go and see.'

Reluctantly Joanna rose to her feet. How could she face Paul again so soon? Why hadn't he taken the dog straight to the Mayfields's house? Perhaps he was injured and that was why he was here. By the time she and Mrs Holman reached the car she saw that was indeed the reason for Paul lifted the heavy dog and went straight across to the surgery. There was nothing for it but to follow him, and, grateful for Mrs Holman's presence, she approached the examination table.

'Where did you find him? Is he hurt?' Mrs Holman asked anxiously as Paul looked up from examining the dog.

'Those woods out on the common near Bayfords' farm,' he said. 'I was doing some pregnancy diagnoses when Mrs Bayford told me a dog had been howling all night. She'd put some food down at the edge of the wood and said she'd caught a glimpse of a large red dog who came towards it but ran away as soon as she approached. He was limping, she said. Half an hour later the food was gone, but there was no further sign of the dog. So then I went to investigate calling Rufus by name, and after a while he came towards me, whimpering and holding up his right forepaw. Luckily he knows me well, so I was able to slip a lead on him.'

All the time he was speaking Paul's eyes were fixed on Mrs Holman, his expression relaxed and friendly, and to Joanna it was plain that he was purposely ignoring her. But he stiffened as she asked suddenly, 'Is the leg broken?'

'No, I don't think so, but I've only given him a cursory examination. I'll hand him over to you now.'

His voice was cold and distant, and, stifling her discomfiture under her usual professional manner, she bent over the dog.

Looking up, she said equally coldly, 'You're right, of

course. The leg is badly bruised—perhaps the car hit it—and he still seems a bit shocked. I'll give him an injection and some tablets to be taken tomorrow, and then I should think the best thing for him would be his own bed at home.'

'I'll take him up, then,' Paul said, but Mrs Holman shook her head. 'Wait a moment. I've just remembered—Mrs Mayfield said they would both be at the hospital for most of the morning. Wouldn't it be a good idea to ring there first?' She paused. 'I'll do it. I've got the hospital number and the name of the ward in my house.'

Left alone with Paul, Joanna stood stroking the dog, her heart beating so fast that she knew she could not endure the cold silence much longer. Looking up, she said, 'Paul—about the story Clare told you—it wasn't true, you know. I didn't——'

'Don't bring that up again,' he interrupted harshly. 'I refuse to discuss it with you.'

'But I must clear myself—you've no right to condemn me out of hand. Please listen. I didn't pressurise——'

Once more he interrupted. 'You can deny it as much as you like, but I don't believe you. Now forget it. I'm going to clean Rufus up.'

She was pale with anger as she watched him comb the long matted coat, and just as she was debating her next move the telephone rang.

'I've been on to the hospital,' said Mrs Holman cheerfully. 'The Mayfields were just leaving, so they immediately went back to tell Clare about Rufus. Will you tell Paul that there's no need for him to take the dog up to their house? They'll pick him up in about twenty minutes.'

As Joanna passed on the message the door opened and Liz came in. 'I've been cleaning out the kennels and Jenny's stall,' she announced, and then went into raptures over Rufus.

After that there was no further opportunity for Joanna to reopen the subject that was uppermost in her mind. Resigned but determined to try again as soon as possible, she went into the office in order to familarise herself with the extra work that would now fall to her lot. Hoping that now Paul would go away, she busied herself until the arrival of the Mayfields, but when she went out to greet them she found to her dismay that he was still in the surgery.

When they had expressed their gratitude to Paul for finding Rufus and Mr Mayfield had examined the dog himself, confirming Joanna's diagnosis, he smiled at her and said, 'I hope you'll come and visit Clare when she's back home again. She'll get very bored with nothing to do all day, so the more people who come the better.'

Mrs Mayfield said thoughtfully, 'Freddy Conway has promised to spend all his free time with her. I'm beginning to hope——'

Her husband laughed. 'I shouldn't bank on anything like that. Clare is very fickle.' He shrugged ruefully. 'I love my daughter dearly, but I've no illusions about her. I know very well that she's made life quite difficult for you all. Up till recently, that is, because since Joanna's arrival she's been much more reasonable.' He smiled. 'You've been a good friend to her, Joanna.'

When the Mayfields left with Rufus Liz went off to lunch and Paul went into the dispensary to refill his case. For a few minutes there was silence, then suddenly Joanna said bitterly, 'I must say Clare has a peculiar way of repaying friendship. Andrew says——' She stopped abruptly as Paul turned swiftly and said angrily,

'What the hell has it to do with Andrew? I would appreciate it if you'd stop discussing me with other people. First of all you encourage Clare to confide in you, then you play on that confidence in order to hurt me and now, it seems, you're stirring things up with Andrew.' Ignoring her gasp of indignation, he went on harshly, 'I wonder what he'd think if he knew what I know about you. That affair with a married man in Suffolk—not your fault, perhaps, but Andrew might not see it that way.' He stopped as she sat down suddenly on a surgery chair, her face deathly pale.

'I'm sorry,' his voice was more gentle. 'Don't worry, I wouldn't dream of hurting him the way you tried to hurt me.'

Suddenly she felt his hand on her shoulder, but she shook him off. 'Please go away.' Her voice was choked. 'Leave me alone.'

'Stop acting like a tragedy queen, then,' he said scornfully and, at that, her temper rose.

'I'm not acting!' she said furiously. 'For heaven's sake, get out of my sight!'

'Very well,' he said coldly, and stood back as she got up to go into the office. Then, just before she shut the door he added, 'Wait. There's one question I must ask you.'

Joanna turned to glare at him. 'I'm not interested in your questions. You've done nothing but torment me ever since I came here.'

She saw his face change and for a moment she was confused at the unmistakable sadness in his eyes. Bewildered, she stared at him for a moment, then she shut the door behind her. A few minutes later she heard his car drive away, leaving her wondering what the question could have been. Well, it was a good thing to have stopped him from asking it—it was probably something to do with the gossip in Suffolk, and that was a subject she had no wish to discuss.

For the next few days, life continued smoothly. Freddy Conway settled down very quickly and it was agreed by everyone that he was an asset to the practice. He came into the surgery on Wednesday morning when Joanna was just finishing operating. Liz looked up as Joanna put in the last suture and said with a grimace, 'A nasty smelly pyometra,' and he smiled but remained silent until the spaniel was installed in a recovery cage. Then as Liz began cleaning up he turned to Joanna.

'Mr Holman has suggested that we should reorganise the small animal emergency calls. He says he doesn't think you're getting enough time off.'

Joanna nodded thoughtfully. 'I suppose that's true. I'm never quite sure who's on duty.'

He grinned. 'I agree—the roster is very muddled. It should be one in four evenings on call for all of us, but, according to Paul, you've been carrying most of the load.'

'Paul said that?'

'Yes, we were discussing it over coffee at the Holmans'.' He laughed. 'I must say, Mrs Holman has a very pleasant set-up there. Tea or coffee on demand and all the latest news.'

'Talking of news—what about Clare?' Liz looked up from wiping the table. 'I've been meaning to visit her in hospital but haven't got round to it yet.'

'I was up there yesterday evening,' Freddy said a little self consciously, and Liz smiled as she glanced quickly at Joanna. 'She told me she's hoping to be home next weekend. She sent her love to you all with an invitation to visit her whenever we like.' He paused, seeing the mischievous gleam in Liz's eyes, and said frankly, 'I know what you're thinking. Yes, I've grown very fond of her.' He hesitated. 'And that's putting it mildly.'

Liz nodded. 'I gathered that from one or two things I've heard. You can't keep secrets in this practice, can you, Joanna?'

Joanna smiled, 'Very true,' and then as the telephone rang she picked up the receiver, glad not to listen to any further talk of Clare. The call was a routine one and while Joanna was giving advice on the feeding of a newly acquired puppy, Freddy left the surgery and Liz gave a quick wave to indicate that she was going over to Mrs Holman's for coffee.

Putting down the receiver, Joanna stood pondering. How soon could she tackle Clare in order to make her own up to Paul? It would be awkward to confront her in her own home under the guise of a friendly visit, but it seemed the only possible way. And if Clare refused—what then? How would Paul ever learn the truth? Throughout the rest of the day her problem remained unsolved, and gradually a feeling of hopelessness crept over her. Perhaps it would be better to abandon the whole idea, although she wanted so desperately to clear herself in Paul's eyes. That evening, however, her spirit rose when she received a call from Mrs Mayfield.

'Clare is asking if you'd go to see her tomorrow evening at the hospital. She's worried about something and seems to think you can help her. I haven't a clue as to what it is—probably nothing very serious, but you know how one exaggerates everything in hospital. I'd be very grateful if you could put her mind at rest.'

Joanna drew a long breath of relief. Once more Clare's conscience seemed to be at work. Perhaps things would come right after all.

Next day Joanna returned to the surgery after making an outside call to find Chrissie agog with news. 'A message from Paul. Apparently Lucky has disappeared. She hasn't touched the food you put down this morning and now Jenny is very restless. When she was taken out for her usual exercise in the yard she kept searching around, and now she's very lethargic and miserable. Paul is coming round to see if Lucky is up in your flat.'

'She's not there—at least I don't think so. She might have got in through an open window when I was out, of course, so I'll go and look.'

There was no sign of the cat, however, and when Joanna arrived back in the surgery she found herself face to face with Paul.

He showed no embarrassment at seeing her again and, taking her cue from him, she said calmly, 'No sign of Lucky upstairs. Where on earth can she have got to?'

'Well, I've looked everywhere. Chrissie has just gone over to the Holmans' to ask if she's been seen round there. That's our last hope.'

Joanna bit her lip. 'I didn't realise this morning that she was missing. I was a bit late and didn't wait for her to come up to me as she usually does. I feel a bit guilty about that.'

Paul frowned. 'Well, you ought to be used to that.'

'What a disgusting thing to say!' Joanna flushed furiously. 'I suppose you think I've hidden Lucky away in order to get even with you. As if I would do such a cruel thing!'

He shrugged. 'Perhaps not, but you must admit——'

It was too much. Her hand flashed out to slap his face but he caught it and held it in a fierce grip. 'All right. No need to be so dramatic. I believe you.' Still he held her hand, then suddenly he drew her towards him and, hypnotised by the open desire in his eyes, she made no resistance. Suddenly the door opened and, as Chrissie appeared, he let her go.

'Good news. Lucky is with Mrs Holman.' Chrissie stopped, glancing curiously from Paul to Joanna. 'Sorry. Have I interrupted something?' She waited for a moment, then went on, 'Lucky was hiding in a corner of the coalshed, but she's been sick and Mrs Holman wants Joanna to come and examine her. She—Lucky—seems quite ill. May have been poisoned.'

Joanna moved swiftly, picking up her case as she went to the door followed by Chrissie carrying a cat basket, and at that moment, the telephone rang.

'OK, I'll deal with it,' Paul said, and picked up the receiver.

Her thoughts on Lucky, Joanna wondered aloud, 'Where on earth could she have picked up poison? She never goes out of the yard.'

Chrissie caught up with her. 'Mrs Holman thinks she must have got out all the same. She probably jumped back over the wall behind the coalshed.' She glanced curiously at Joanna. 'By the way, whatever was going on between you and Paul back there in the surgery? He looked awfully strange and you seemed almost dazed.'

Joanna managed to shrug lightly. 'We had a bit of a disagreement, that's all. Paul and I don't get on very well, you know.'

Chrissie looked sceptical. 'That's funny. I could have sworn that Paul——' She paused. 'Mark says——'

'Oh, do shut up, Chrissie,' Joanna said irritably. 'I've

got more important things on my mind at the moment than
to listen to what Mark thinks.'

'Sorry,' Chrissie said humbly, and Joanna instantly
regretted having snubbed her. But it was the only way to
protect herself from being talked about. She would like to
have known what it was that Mark said about Paul, but it
would be foolish to enquire. A few minutes later, as she
gazed down at Lucky, her heart sank.

'She's been sick again,' said Mrs Holman. 'Evil-smelling
stuff—fishy.'

Joanna studied her thermometer. 'Subnormal,' she said
heavily. 'Let's get her into the basket and back to the surgery
as quickly as possible.'

Paul was still there when they entered and Chrissie briefly
described Lucky's condition while Joanna went into the
dispensary. She came out with a bottle of liquid and said,
'I'll have to give her this mixture to settle the stomach and
stop the sickness. She'll probably bring the first dose back
but, hopefully, she'll keep most of the second one down. If
tomorrow she takes a little milk and her temperature comes
up to normal then she'll be OK. Otherwise——' She shook
her head. 'I blame myself in a way. I ought to have brought
her in every night.'

'Nonsense!' Paul said sharply. 'It wouldn't have made
any difference at all. Cats like their freedom and nothing will
stop them when they get the urge to roam. By the way, I've
been talking to the donkey sanctuary people and they're
willing to take Jenny in a fortnight's time. The farrier down
there will continue the work that has been done here. I
mentioned Lucky and, subject to your consent, they'd like to
take her too. Lots of their donkeys have particular friends.
One has a goat to which he's very attached and they say that
Jenny will settle down much more quickly if Lucky is with
her. Would you mind?'

'Of course I wouldn't. Lucky won't miss me and I've seen
very little of her. But it remains to be seen if—' Joanna
nodded towards the cat. 'Look out, Chrissie, that dose is

coming back!'

But some of it remained, and eventually the second dose was given and retained. Joanna's hopes rose. Watched over carefully, it looked as though Lucky would recover and would be better in the morning. Then suddenly she remembered the visit this evening to Clare. Well, that would have to wait. Lucky could not be neglected, the medicine must be continued and the next few hours would be critical. It seemed as though Fate had stepped in to prevent the showdown with Clare.

Her supposition, however, was proved to be wrong when, a short time later, Freddy entered the surgery.

'Mrs Holman told me about Lucky and I know that Clare is hoping to see you this evening, so if you like, I'll do the surgery, keep an eye on Lucky and remain here till you get back.'

Rather reluctantly Joanna agreed and, after discussing the treatment being given, Freddy said, 'Give my love to Clare. I hope you'll be able to cheer her up—I don't like to see her unhappy.'

'Is she unhappy?' Joanna asked carefully. 'Don't you think it might just be depression brought on by her accident? After all, she's broken her leg and had a nasty shock—I shouldn't worry too much if I were you.'

'Perhaps you're right.' Freddy looked relieved. 'Anyhow, she'll be pleased to see you—she's very fond of you.'

Joanna smiled wryly to herself as she drove to the hospital. Clare had a strange way of showing her affection. So self-absorbed that she never considered other people's feelings, she seemed to have no scruples about the harm she did by telling lies.

Seeing the quantity of flowers round Clare's bed Joanna felt rather guilty at having come with empty hands. But, reminding herself of Clare's mischiefmaking, she greeted her coolly. After a few minutes' stiff conversation during which Joanna searched for the appropriate moment in which to make her demand, Clare shifted uneasily on her pillows and stared down at her plastered leg. Then suddenly she said defiantly,

'All right, Joanna. I know you're angry with me and that I shouldn't have pretended to Paul that you forced me to tell him I was responsible for breaking up his affair with Fiona. But I was so nervous of telling him that it seemed the best way to prevent his getting angry. You see, when I'd told him, he asked me why I had left it so long. Was it because I wanted to rub salt into the wound now that it was too late to do anything about it? I said I wanted to straighten things out—that my conscience was hurting me—but he didn't believe me. I was just naturally cruel, he said. That was so unfair that I said I hadn't wanted to hurt him but that you'd made me realise it was the right thing to do. It seemed to work, because he said then that I was just a silly little fool and that I ought to have realised that you were just using me to get at him. I asked him not to say anything to you, but he said he'd have it out with you.'

Joanna tried to keep the contempt out of her voice but only partially succeeded. 'So you expect me to let him go on thinking it was my idea?'

'Why not? It isn't as if Paul's opinion means anything to you. You see—' Clare gazed up appealingly, 'if it came out that I was lying again Paul might be so angry that he might tell Freddy, and I simply couldn't bear that.' She began to cry weakly, and as the tears fell Joanna's anger gave way to pity. Pity for the silly mixed-up girl who was so callous about other people's feelings and who was now so bitterly afraid of the possible consequences. 'Don't get upset,' she took hold of Clare's hand, 'Paul would never do that. He's not the type. So you've nothing to fear when you tell him the truth. You really must, Clare. It's not fair to me.'

Clare shook her head obstinately. 'I can't go through all that again. It simply doesn't matter—you and Paul hate the sight of each other, so there's no harm done.'

'But there is,' Joanna stared at her in dismay. 'You can't just leave it at that!'

Clare wiped her eyes and said sullenly, 'You've no right to worry me like this. I can feel my temperature going up.'

'I'm sorry,' Joanna was forced to acknowledge defeat, 'we'd better leave it for the moment. But will you promise to think it over? Please—for my sake if not for your own.'

'I don't expect I'll change my mind,' Clare said ungraciously, and turned her head away as Joanna said goodbye.

Driving home, she tried to come to terms with the fact that she must resign herself to Paul's continued contempt. It would be hard to endure, but she would have to live with it unless she could manage to convince him herself. She must seize any opportunity that came her way, though in his present frame of mind, it would be difficult to make him listen. Better to wait until his anger had cooled.

Freddy greeted her cheerfully on her return to the surgery.

'Lucky's going to be OK. The sickness has stopped, she's keeping down the medicine and her temperature is coming up.' He paused and added eagerly, 'How's Clare?'

Joanna smiled, 'She's OK too,' and added a little white lie, 'she sent you her love.'

He left shortly after and as Joanna saw him out she caught sight of Paul coming up the yard. Turning back quickly, she hoped he hadn't seen her, but it was too late. 'How's Lucky?' he asked as he drew near, and with an effort Joanna spoke calmly. 'Going to be all right, I think. How's Jenny?'

'A bit melancholy.' Paul stood at the open surgery door, 'but her feet are showing improvement.' There was a long silence and Joanna was just on the point of turning away when he said suddenly, 'Will you come with me when we take her to the sanctuary?'

Stunned, Joanna opened her eyes wide in astonishment. For a moment she was speechless, then she said angrily, 'After all the things you called me, condemned me out of hand—I must say, I think you've got a nerve! You know I very much wanted to go with you, but now we're too much

at loggerheads to spend even ten minutes together without a
blazing row.'

His eyes darkened and his mouth hardened. Then
suddenly he relaxed and grinned apologetically. 'I'm sorry, I
went too far. Will you forgive and forget?' He put out his
hand and stood waiting.

It took a few seconds for Joanna to recover herself, then
slowly she put her hand in his and in spite of the way in
which her heart was pounding she said lightly, 'Yes, of
course. Professionally at least we're on the same
wavelength.'

There was a glint in the grey eyes and his mouth twitched
at the corner. 'Right. The weekend after next—that's when
the farrier will transport Jenny. We'll go in my car. With
Lucky, if she is OK by then. Are you still willing to
relinquish her?'

'Oh, yes, if you think she'll be happy there.'

'No doubt about that. A peculiar friendship, but it's very
touching. Animals are strange creatures. Which reminds
me—' he paused, then added hesitatingly, 'I have to call at
the zoo at Waybourne this week to take the entropian
sutures out of the tigress. Would you like to come? It would
be after your morning surgery. They've asked me to be their
regular vet and I've agreed, though actually I hate zoos. But
someone must look after the unfortunate inmates and it's all
good experience.'

'I'd love to come.' Joanna's eyes shone and when Paul
had gone the pleasant feeling stayed with her as she went
back into the surgery.

That night she went to bed with a heart that was
considerably lighter. Going out with Paul might well lead to
an opportunity to put things straight with him, but she must
choose the right moment carefully in order to avoid another
furious quarrel.

He came into the surgery on Wednesday morning, but
she ignored his presence, bending over a patient on the table
in a way that showed him an emergency had occurred. He

stood waiting silently, watching her trying to revive a small dog, and Liz glanced his way and shrugged her shoulders hopelessly.

At last Joanna gave up and turned away from the table. 'It's no good,' her voice was choked—'I've tried everything. He's gone.' Taking out her handkerchief, she went quickly into the dispensary and Liz, looking down at the pathetic little body on the table said, 'It was awful. He's only a young dog, but as soon as he'd had the first small dose of anaesthetic he went out like a light. I've never seen anything like it. No question of a full dose of anaesthetic—we couldn't believe it.' She stopped as the telephone rang and went into the office to take the call.

Going into the dispensary, Paul put an arm round Joanna's shoulders and for a minute she stood very still, grateful for his comforting presence. Then, gently releasing herself, she said shakily, 'I suppose it's one of these very rare cases where the patient is absolutely allergic to anaesthetic. There was no way of knowing in advance. Have you ever had it happen to a patient of yours?'

'No, but soon after I qualified it happened to a colleague of mine. A young dog too—very highly strung. It's one of those things, you know. You're not to blame in any way.'

'All the same,' Joanna blinked hard, 'I feel like a murderer. I must go and tell the owner.'

'Would you like me to telephone for you?' he asked, but Joanna shook her head.

'That would be cowardly. I must do it myself.'

A good ten minutes later she came out of the office, her eyes still wet with tears, and Paul pointed to the coffee Liz was pouring out. 'Plenty of time. Drink that first. You need it.'

Silently she sat down and meeting his sympathetic gaze she said slowly, 'Mrs Bradley, the owner, is in a terrible state. Practically hysterical and blaming me. She says she's going to take it up with the Royal College of Veterinary Surgeons.' She took a quick gulp of coffee, then added shakily, 'I'm terrified. I've never had that threat before.'

'Now don't get worried,' Paul's voice was calm. 'The Royal College will understand the situation. My friend had the same experience and he was completely exonerated. Your client will probably receive an explanatory letter from them and you'll be informed that they've sent it. That is if she ever does report it. It is, as I said, one of those things.' He saw her wince, and added quickly, 'I'm not being callous. It's true.' He paused. 'Now come with me to this little zoo. Liz will hold the fort and it will take you out of yourself.'

Liz nodded. 'That's right. I'll ring you if anything comes in that I can't deal with, but I don't expect that to happen.'

Joanna looked at her doubtfully. 'You mean if Mrs Bradley should come in?'

Liz nodded. 'I shouldn't think it's likely, but in any case we'll all back you up.'

It was a silent journey with Joanna deep in gloomy thought, but as Paul pulled up outside the zoo gates she drew a long breath and said slowly, 'I suppose you think I'm an awful fool.'

'Of course I don't. It was a horrible experience.' He paused, then added thoughtfully, 'Do you remember the other evening when you and Andrew were watching me trying to save that stray dog? I said then that I would rather try to comfort a weeping animal owner than have to cope with the heartbroken mother of a dead child. Think of that. It should help you to get things in proportion.'

She looked at him, her eyes full of gratitude, and he laid his hand on hers. At his touch a great glow of love enveloped her whole being and as he got out of the car to open the gates she sat for a few moments as though in a trance.

CHAPTER EIGHT

AS THEY drove up to a large, sprawling house Paul explained that the place had been originally run as a restaurant but the new owners had expanded it by putting swings and slides for children in the large grounds. Then they had added a miniature zoo which had proved a great attraction. They began with a large aviary, a few cages of monkeys and a sort of children's corner with a pony for rides, a mouse village and half a dozen sheep. It had become so popular that they had decided to go in for more exotic creatures—hence the tigers. Paul paused in his explanation as they drew up outside the house and sat for a moment in silence. At last he said thoughtfully, 'Personally, I think they've gone a bit over the top. I know they've got a good keeper—that man who brought Chloe into the surgery—and his nephew assists him, but tigers are a terrific responsibility. Far better to keep to the smaller, less dangerous animals. I've told them what I think and I'm hoping they'll eventually sell the tigers to a larger zoo.'

As they approached the front door Joanna said, 'Those sutures—can you take them out without an anaesthetic?'

'I hope so,' Paul laughed. 'I gave George instructions to dope Chloe with tranquillisers. It will only take a few seconds and she's still fairly docile. Anyhow, we'll see.'

Mr and Mrs Betheridge welcomed them in and immediately offered tea, but Paul said, 'Well, I'd rather take out the stitches first. I must make sure that Chloe's eye is now normal. After that, will you show us round your zoo? My colleague here is very interested.'

George, standing by the large cage, looked rather anxious.

'She's pretty dopey,' he said, 'but I'm a bit dubious. Are you sure you want to do it like this?'

137

'Don't worry,' Paul said easily, 'I'm sure it will be OK. I don't want to give her a full anaesthetic so soon after the last one.'

Suddenly, as they gathered round the cage, Chloe half rose to her feet and her lips lifted in a small snarl. Then, once more, she subsided on to the floor.

'My nephew's here,' George pointed to a large young man who appeared in the doorway, 'he's very strong and will help to hold her.'

'I can help too if necessary,' said Mr Betheridge, 'though I must admit I'd rather not.' He laughed nervously and stepped back as though he rather regretted having offered.

The cage door was opened very quietly and George and Paul approached slowly, George murmuring soothing words as Chloe lifted her head suspiciously. Then gently stroking her he kept her head still long enough for Paul to snip out the sutures. Apart from another little snarl she seemed not to notice and, with one long searching look at the eye, Paul nodded his head and came out of the cage.

'It looks terribly bruised and puffy,' said Mrs Betheridge doubtfully, but he reassured her.

'It's fine. In a few days' time that bruising will have gone. It's very successful—the eye is normal now.' He paused. 'She mustn't return to the others until all the after-effects have gone.'

George grinned ruefully. 'She'll be a handful to look after. She's dopey now, but when that wears off she'll show her displeasure in no uncertain way. She doesn't like being kept in that cage.'

'Neither would I,' said Paul sharply, and turned to the Betheridges. 'Quite frankly I hate the idea of these large wild creatures being confined. That enclosure you've got outside is quite good but, in my opinion, it isn't really large enough. Have you thought of the future? These tigers are not yet fully grown.'

'Yes,' Mrs Betheridge nodded ruefully, 'we've begun to realise we've been a bit too ambitious. We've made a few

enquiries and as soon as Chloe is ready we're going to sell
them all to a much bigger zoo where they'll have more
space.'

George said with obvious relief, 'Thank goodness for
that,' then added, 'I've got a bit of a problem with the
porcupines. The female has had some young—her second
lot—and just like the first time, she's eaten them. Why on
earth should she do that?'

Paul looked thoughtful. 'I think the answer is that she's
probably lacking in calcium. Those hard spines need a lot to
harden them. I suggest you give her bones to eat and plenty
of milk.'

'Problems—problems——' Mrs Betheridge seemed
depressed. Turning on Joanna, 'Well, come and see the rest
of our menagerie.'

As they went outside, Mr Betheridge said, 'The monkeys
are worrying us too. We've taken your advice, Mr
Copeland, and you'll see now that they're properly housed.
We've got them in the open air with heated dens for them to
sleep in at night, but as you told us, they're very delicate and
subject to infections of all kinds. The trouble is they're
always fighting and get lots of bites and cuts.'

Paul nodded. 'You'll have to keep a constant watch,
because those bites nearly always turn septic. That little
fellow over there—he's got a bite on his right shoulder,
hasn't he?'

'Yes,' George admitted, 'he was in a fight yesterday.
What do you advise?'

Paul went up to the bars and examined the monkey
closely. 'It looks a bit nasty. You'd better isolate him for a
few days and I'll give you some antibiotic to put in his
drinking water. But you can't keep him isolated for more
than a few days or the rest of the troop won't accept him
when he goes back.'

'I really think,' Mrs Betheridge sighed heavily, 'we've
taken on a bit too much. We're doing very well financially,
but sometimes when I see children shouting and trying to

tease the animals I wonder if this idea of a small zoo is a good one after all.'

Joanna looked sympathetic. 'I know how you feel. Mind you, this children's corner is nice—that ought to be enough to amuse small children.'

Mrs Betheridge nodded. 'But now my husband is talking of a reptile house. What do you think about that?'

Joanna repressed a shudder. 'Frankly, reptiles give me the horrors, but that's purely personal, and children seem to like things that make their flesh creep.' She caught sight of a signal from Paul. 'I think it's time we were going.'

On the way back Paul said vehemently, 'I really do hate zoos, don't you? Those monkeys, right out of their natural element—the tigers, the birds—ah well. Let's talk of something more pleasant. How about a snack lunch in a pub? There's a nice little place down the lane.'

Settled at a table by a window, Paul said, 'What do you think of this idea about reorganising the practice?'

'Reorganising—oh, you mean time off—sticking to the roster?'

'No. There's much more to it than that.' Paul pushed his plate aside. 'Freddy Conway and Mr Mayfield have got together and decided that we're behind the times and must modernise.'

Joanna stared. 'What on earth will that entail? I thought we were modern enough already—a bit disorganised perhaps, but that can easily be remedied. Where did you hear all this?'

'Mr Mayfield told me. I went to see Clare the other evening and he and I had a long talk afterwards. There's going to be a meeting next week at the Mayfields' house and we all have to go. Apparently Freddy, having come from a large, very efficient practice, has stung the partners into action. It's all about competition, making the practice more profitable—it's not my cup of tea at all.'

Joanna sat in silence for a few minutes while Paul gazed moodily out of the window. At last she said, 'I agree with you. Veterinary surgery is not about getting richer and richer. I know there's a lot of competition, but surely this practice is strong enough and profitable enough as it is. Anyway, what exactly are they planning?'

Paul turned to face her. 'A lot of rebuilding. The reception area to be enlarged, a bigger car park, a display unit for merchandise so that clients can buy pet foods, flea collars, vitamin tablets—you name it. Under new legislation this is now permitted. Another operating theatre, a new recovery ward, sliding doors between rooms such as the surgery and the dispensary. A consulting room, lots of new equipment, etc. Of course it will all be marvellous from the point of view of impressing the clients and—' he shrugged cynically, 'the fees will go up accordingly. There'll be more staff, a full-time secretary, another couple of veterinary nurses—probably even two more vets.' He gazed down into his glass. 'To me it's a sign that my time here is up.'

Joanna stared at him. 'What on earth——? They're surely not going to sack you!'

'No,' he gave a short laugh, 'Mr Mayfield has renewed his offer of a partnership. Of course, it would be well worth my while financially, but—' he shook his head—'I thanked him but told him I'm go ng to put up my plate in Suffolk.'

A large lump rose in Joanna's throat and she found herself unable to speak. She stared down at the table, knowing that, if she looked up, Paul would see the dismay she could not conceal.

Suddenly, irrelevantly, he said softly, 'Your eyelashes throw a shadow on your cheeks like soft, dark wings.'

This was so unlike him that she glanced up startled and saw something in his expression that sent a tremor right through her. Swallowing hard, she ignored the compliment and said evenly, 'I don't suppose Mr Mayfield was best pleased at your decision.'

He shrugged. 'He'll have no difficulty in replacing me. I don't know whether Mark will stay, but Freddy—ah!' he laughed. 'Well, he'll certainly become a partner. Clare will see to that.'

'Do you think he and Clare——' Joanna stopped. She had no wish to talk of Clare right now. But it was too late. Paul took up the subject.

'Oh, yes. It's almost a foregone conclusion. Apparent to everyone, which brings me to something I ought to have said before.' He paused, flushing a little under his tan. 'I owe you a very abject apology. I went to see Clare with one object in view and I got the result I hoped for. I made her admit that she had lied about you. I knew it subconsciously, but at the time I was so angry about the whole thing that I couldn't stop calling you all the names under the sun.' He frowned and passed his hand through his hair in a gesture of embarrassment that to Joanna was infinitely touching. 'Will you forgive me, please? I behaved disgustingly. Don't let me leave the practice without your forgiveness.'

Conscious of a dull ache in her heart, Joanna tried to speak lightly. 'Of course I forgive you, and I'm awfully glad you managed to get the truth out of Clare. I tried, but she wouldn't co-operate.' Smiling, she put out her hand and he gripped it tightly. For a few moments she gave herself up to the pleasure of contact with him, then in an endeavour to stop the inevitable she said, 'Why not stay in the practice a little longer? Take up Mr Mayfield's offer of a partnership and benefit financially. You could always be bought out after a few years and then you would have enough capital to set up on your own.'

Paul sat in silence, gazing at her reflectively. At last he said, 'I've got enough capital now to set up in a quiet way in Suffolk, and I want to do that more than anything. I like the idea of gradually building up a practice entirely by my own efforts. Build it up by personal recommendation until it will stand an assistant who will eventually become a partner and then stay at that. I'm not the kind of vet to be part of a commercial enterprise. I don't want an empire of small branches—because that's what will happen here, you know, in spite of what they say at the moment. I shan't mind if

in Suffolk I'm surrounded by competition. If I'm good
enough I'll hold my own. My fees will be moderate because
I shan't have the enormous expenses of a large practice, and
I have this conviction that pet owners and farmers should not
be penalised by high fees which might well prevent them
from giving their animals the medical care they need.'

It was a picture that made Joanna's heart glow with
sympathy. An idealistic vision which would mean hard work
and dedication in order to survive the first few years.

She said as much and he nodded in agreement. 'Yes,
you've summed it up correctly. At first there wouldn't be
much spare time, on call twenty-four hours a day, but it
wouldn't be long before I could take on extra help.'

He stopped and Joanna sat in silence visualising the
future. A future which suddenly seemed empty and grey.

Paul's voice broke in on her depression. 'I'm afraid I'm
boring you with my castles in the air. I've been accused of
that before, you know.' He spoke lightly, but there was a
chill in his words, and Joanna frowned.

'But it isn't true,' she said firmly. 'You know now that
Clare made it up. Your—what was her name?—yes, Fiona
was never bored—she found your conversation fascinating.'

'Maybe,' he said drily, 'but you told me once that you
didn't want to hear any more about Suffolk. In other words,
I was boring you stiff.'

'No, you weren't. That wasn't the reason. It was
because——' Joanna stopped abruptly and felt her face grow
hot as she saw from the expression in Paul's eyes that he had
read her thoughts. Glancing quickly at her watch, she said
hastily, 'Don't you think we ought to be getting back?'

'Another few minutes,' he said smoothly. 'I begin to
understand your reason for disliking Suffolk, but I would
like to know the truth about your affair. I've only heard a lot
of garbled stories passed on to my sister.'

Joanna's hands clenched involuntarily. 'Well, you'll have
to be content with that,' she snapped. 'I don't want to talk
about the past. It's dead and gone.'

'Like your former lover.' Paul's voice was hard. 'He was drowned, wasn't he? And that's why you hate the sea.'

'He wasn't my lover!' Joanna's eyes blazed for a moment, then she went on recklessly not caring, now that he had pierced through the reserve that prevented her from talking of the past, 'I loved him, yes—at least, I thought I did—but I never—we never——' She stopped, choked with anger at the cynical disbelief in his eyes.

'His wife seemed to think——' he said softly. His voice was gentle, but incredulity lingered in his glance, infuriating Joanna so much that she defended herself passionately.

'I don't care what his wife thought. She never gave me the benefit of the doubt. I've said it a hundred times and I'll say it again—I never knew he was married.'

'Ah!' Paul leaned back in his chair and sighed as though with relief. Gazing at her thoughtfully, he said, 'So that's the real story. The one that people refused to believe.'

'Yes,' she said emphatically, 'the truth. Now stop talking about it, please.' Exhausted by her vehemence, Joanna lifted her glass with shaking hands, not even noticing that it was empty.

'Let me get you another drink,' he said, but she shook her head.

'No, thank you. Let's go now.'

He said very little on the way back and Joanna, immersed in thoughts that were half resentful, half glad that at last he knew the truth, did nothing to break the silence. What difference, she wondered, did it make, after all? It was probably only idle curiosity that had prompted his questioning—curiosity aroused by his sister who was quite likely one of those people who had whispered about her so maliciously.

As they pulled up outside the yard gates Paul spoke at last.

'Shall we say next Sunday for the donkey sanctuary?'

About to agree, Joanna suddenly hesitated. How could she spend a whole day in Paul's company without betraying the fact that she loved him? Now that he had decided to leave the practice would it not be better to avoid any close companionship that must inevitably end in sadness?

'Now look here, Joanna—' his voice was impatient—'you said you'd like to go, so why are you looking so doubtful?'

Seeking wildly for an excuse, she said, 'I really don't like being away from the surgery for a long time—even on a Sunday.'

'Is that so? Then what about the time you went out with Andrew? You had no such qualms then.' He shrugged. 'It comes back to the same old thing, doesn't it? You can't stand my company for very long.'

Once more, to Joanna's dismay, she saw that the situation was beginning to get out of control and, confused, she said as calmly as she could, 'That's not quite true. This afternoon I've enjoyed being out with you, but you know as well as I do that we often quarrel violently.'

He turned and gave her a long, steady look. 'There could be a reason for that.'

'What kind of reason?' Her pounding heart told her the reason for her own reaction to his presence, but she managed to speak calmly, almost indifferently.

'I just said there *could* be a reason, but I can't fathom the workings of your feminine mind and I wouldn't like to guess wrongly.'

'Goodness!' She achieved a touch of light mockery. 'You sound very profound—too profound for my poor feminine mind to comprehend.'

'Stop it, Joanna!' Paul said harshly. 'We're not playing a game. At least, I'm not.' He drew a long, exasperated breath. 'Let's get back to what I asked you. Will you come or not?'

Hastily she pushed aside her doubts. Why not enjoy a few hours with him? So long as she kept the atmosphere light and friendly there need be no quarrelsome arguments. 'All right,' she said at last, 'I'll come just so long as no emergency gets in the way.'

'Right,' he sounded satisfied, 'I'll arrange with the

farrier and let you know when I'll pick you up.'

Evening surgery over, Joanna made her weekly call to her parents. As always they were interested in her work and, after regaling them with various anecdotes she was about to ring off when her mother said, 'We're longing to see you again. When are you coming for a weekend?'

Remorsefully Joanna knew that, subconsciously, she had been avoiding that question, and impulsively she said, 'I'll try and make it the weekend after next.'

Pleased at her mother's joyful reaction, she put down the receiver then, almost immediately, regretted her impetuous decision. How could she take that weekend off when she had already arranged to go to the donkey sanctuary this coming Sunday? But that was only one day—she could probably fix it for the following weekend. Resolved not to disappoint her parents, she pushed the matter firmly to the back of her mind.

It was only when she got into Paul's car on Sunday morning that it came once more to the fore. Putting Lucky's basket in the back of the car, Paul said, 'I feel rather guilty about taking her away from you, but I have a solution which I hope will make up for it. I know where there's a good litter of puppies—springer spaniels. Will you let me give you one?'

'A puppy? Oh, how lovely!' Joanna exclaimed impulsively, then as his last words sank in she said, 'But I can't let you give it to me. I'll buy it myself.' Seeing his face darken, she added hastily, 'You mustn't think I feel sad at losing Lucky. She quite plainly prefers Jenny's company to mine.'

'That's true. Listen to her now. Those miaows are angry protests at being so forcibly separated from her. She'll be overjoyed when she sees her again and won't give you another thought.'

Joanna laughed, then she asked casually, 'Where is the litter of puppies? Is it local—one of your clients?'

'No, it's a good way away. I thought perhaps we could

go and look at it together. The puppies will be too young to leave their mother, but at least you could make your choice. He paused. 'What about the weekend after next?'

'The weekend after next? Oh, but I was thinking of going to see my parents that weekend. I don't want to disappoint them.'

He laughed easily. 'No need to change your plans. The litter is in Suffolk. My sister's English springer spaniel bitch—I can vouch for their breeding. I have a few days' holiday due to me, so I can get away then. I'll drive you down.'

Joanna's heart seemed to lurch. Go to Suffolk with Paul—meet his sister—oh, no! Frantically she tried to think of a way out, but her mind went blank. At last, trying to keep the tension out of her voice, she said, 'I don't think that will be possible. I shall need my car when I'm home and once there it won't be easy to get away. My mother has all sorts of things planned.'

There was a long silence, then he burst out angrily, 'Just another excuse to avoid my company!' He drew a long breath. 'Well if you'll trust my judgment I'll choose a puppy for you. Which would you prefer—a dog or a bitch?'

'A dog, please. Yes, I'll certainly trust your judgment, but I insist on paying for it myself.' Glancing at him quickly, she saw such a hurt expression in his eyes that she relented. 'Look—I've changed my mind. I won't drive down with you because I really will need my own car, but if you like, I'll meet you there and see the puppies myself.'

'That's better,' he said approvingly. 'Let me have your parents' telephone number so that I can ring you in order to fix the time.'

For the rest of the journey Joanna tried not to think of the decision she had taken. Later, she felt sure, she would begin to worry and possibly regret it but, for the moment, it must be forgotten.

On arrival at the donkey sanctuary Paul introduced her to Mr and Mrs Richardson, the middle-aged couple who owned and ran the place, and their dedication to their work of mercy was so evident that she felt instantly drawn towards them. Paul, having already seen everything, volunteered to show her round, and as they covered the large acreage her heart warmed at the sight of the happy little donkeys enjoying a life of special care and love. So many of them, she was told, had suffered badly from neglect, been so lonely and often ill-treated, that this refuge must have seemed like heaven to them when they arrived. As she stood scratching inside the ear of one elderly donkey whose eyes were half closed in sheer enjoyment of its favourite caress, she listened to its life story told by Paul in such a moving way that tears came into her eyes. At last he said, 'Let's go over to the hospital. I'd like you to meet Dick Archer. He's the vet I told you about and when Jenny arrives he'll give her a thorough examination.'

Fully equipped and well organised the hospital was absorbing, and the two cheerful veterinary nurses made her welcome until Dick Archer arrived. A tall, fair-haired, round-faced man of about thirty, he greeted Paul jovially then, on being introduced to Joanna, he fell silent, gazing at her in such open admiration that she had difficulty in suppressing laughter.

'You lucky devil!' He turned at last to Paul with a broad grin. 'Imagine having such a lovely colleague. How can you possibly concentrate on your work when she's around?'

Paul's mouth twitched at the corner and Joanna's mirth came to the surface. 'You little know,' she said mockingly. 'Paul and I have only one thing in common and that is our profession. The rest of the time we seem to spend fighting.'

'Good lord! I don't believe it! Paul, you must be mad! Much as I love my work here I'd change places with you any day, and I bet I wouldn't fight with you, Joanna.' Dick paused and his grin grew broader. 'Well, if there's no competition I'll have to find my way up to your practice and try my luck.'

'No chance for you there,' Paul's voice was suddenly

cynical, 'she's more interested in the local doctor.'

Joanna flushed, bit her lip angrily, and turned to chat with the amused veterinary nurses. Then, to her relief, Mrs Richardson came in.

'Your donkey has arrived. I understand you've brought a cat who's devoted to her. Will you get her and we'll put the two of them together in a stable to settle down for a while.'

Lucky, released from her prison, looked very suspicious as Joanna carried her to the stable and protested loudly in fierce wails of indignation as they stood waiting for Jenny to come down the ramp of the horsebox.

Dick Archer frowned at the sight of her misshapen feet and Paul, glancing at him quickly, said, 'You should have seen her before our farrier got to work. She's vastly improved.'

'Don't worry,' Dick recognised the anxiety in Paul's voice, 'I've seen one or two cases as bad as hers. I'm fairly confident that our farrier who specialises in donkeys will get her right. Nearly right, anyhow. Well enough to enjoy life here, anyway.'

Slowly and carefully Jenny was led into the stable and for a few moments the little donkey stood, head down, looking as mournful as the first time Joanna had seen her. Then, suddenly, there was a loud miaow from Lucky and struggling fiercely in Joanna's arms she fought to be put down. Immediately Jenny lifted her head and her eyes grew bright with recognition as Lucky was placed in the straw at her feet. Purring loudly, the cat walked round and round her friend, finally settling down beside her.

It was so touching that a lump came into Joanna's throat, then, as she looked at the smiling faces around her, she asked, 'What will happen to Lucky when Jenny eventually goes out to join the others?'

Mrs Richardson laughed. 'She'll be all right. She'll probably always stay near Jenny when she's under cover, and she'll also build up a life of her own. A very useful one to us—she'll help keep the mice down. We've several cats here and they're all very contented.'

They waited for a while as Jenny was watered and fed and Lucky was given a bowl of milk, then Dick turned to Paul. 'I've studied the information you've given me and I see that Jenny's injections are up to date, so all she'll need is our usual treatment for a newcomer. You know, examination, blood sample, worming and a dung count.' He paused. 'I must go now, but you'll come again, won't you?' He grinned mischievously at Joanna. 'Remember me if you get tired of your doctor friend.'

When he had gone Joanna said crossly, 'I wish you wouldn't link me with Andrew like that. You know very well that I'm not serious about him.'

Paul shrugged almost indifferently. 'Well, I didn't want to encourage Dick. He was obviously very interested in you.' Ignoring her puzzled stare, he looked at his watch. 'We'd better be on our way if we want to get lunch in a pub. I spotted a nice one on our way here.'

As they left he said, 'I shall miss that little donkey, but that's the worst of becoming attached to a patient.'

'She couldn't be in a better place,' Joanna said comfortingly. 'It's lovely to see people who really care for animals in such a practical way.'

They were having lunch when suddenly Paul said, 'I've been thinking about this puppy business. I haven't forced it on you, have I? I mean, there's no particular reason why you should have to have a springer spaniel. You might prefer another breed. If so, don't hesitate to say so.'

Quickly Joanna realised that here was her chance to avoid getting involved in a situation from which she instinctively recoiled. Knowing now that Paul was definitely going to leave the practice, she must put him out of her mind, and already she was regretting her rash decision to meet him in Suffolk. She drew a long breath. 'Well, I've been thinking too,' she said, and saw with a sharp pang the cynical look return to his eyes. 'It's not that I don't want a springer spaniel—I love them—but it will be a bit difficult for me to look after it properly. Things are going to be a bit hectic now that Clare has left.'

To her surprise he seemed to understand. 'Quite true. Perhaps it would be wise to wait a few months.' He said nothing for a minute, then he added, 'I've got an idea. You could select the puppy you want and my sister could keep it for you till it's about six months old. I know she wouldn't mind—if she had her way she'd keep the lot, but she knows that's not very practical.'

This was even worse. Desperately Joanna tried again. She shook her head. 'It's very kind of you, but really, I think we'd better forget the whole idea. I'll wait until the time when I can commit myself fully to taking on a dog and I don't really know when that will be. My plans might change—I feel rather unsettled at the moment.'

'Your plans?' For a moment Paul looked startled, then he shrugged. 'Well, of course that's quite likely. You might get married. Andrew—no?' he saw her angry frown. 'Well, anyone—Dick Archer—' he laughed a little grimly. 'He was properly floored, wasn't he? Anyway, you'll certainly have no difficulty if marriage is your objective.'

'Marriage is not my objective,' she took him up sharply, 'I'm talking of my professional future. I may want to move on like you.' She paused. 'I don't know what I want to do exactly, but I've come to the conclusion that I don't want to stay in the practice for ever, especially in view of all the changes that are in the offing.'

Paul's face changed. His cynical smile softened to one of genuine interest. 'Do you regret having turned down Mr Bridges' offer of a partnership?'

She nodded slowly. 'Sometimes I do, but it was so painful after—' she stopped as she saw his eyes narrow—'well, you know what I mean. So I ran away. Ran away from the malicious gossip and my own unhappiness.'

There was a long silence. She lowered her eyes, burning now with unshed tears, but she could feel the intensity of Paul's gaze as he sat waiting for her next words. At last she looked up. 'I could never go back there to live permanently. Suffolk—the North Sea——' she shuddered. 'I'll always hate that part of the world.'

He frowned, then suddenly, irrelevantly, he said, 'My father was a fighter pilot in the war. He flew Spitfires and had some terrible experiences. One thing he told me has always stayed in my mind. He was shot up but managed to get his plane back to England and crashed in a field. He got out safely with a couple of broken ribs, but found that his nerve had gone. He asked to be transferred to ground staff, but was told that the only way to conquer his fear was to fly again as soon as possible. Which, very much against his will, he did. He regained his confidence and ended up the war with a DFC and bar.'

Joanna let her breath out slowly. 'Are you telling me that I ought to have stayed with Mr Bridges? Carried on as usual—gone sailing with someone else—stayed to face the music in fact?'

'Well, no, not exactly. You've widened your experience in another practice—a good thing in itself—and probably come to terms with your lover's deceit. But in order to exorcise the past completely you should go back to Suffolk—a holiday perhaps—or better still take another job there if you don't want to go back to Mr Bridges.'

One word of his calm advice stood out from the others, and Joanna pounced on it angrily. 'James was *not* my lover! How many times do I have to say that? I admit I was considering giving in to him, but—' she shrugged unhappily, 'Fate stepped in and he was drowned.'

'Just in time, then,' Paul said callously, and staring at him indignantly, she began to regret having told him so much of her hitherto well hidden feelings. Putting her thoughts into words, she said,

'I can't think why I've been so talkative. It must be very boring for you to listen to my—' she laughed self-mockingly, ''my purple past.''

He gave her a lopsided grin. 'Hardly purple. Green

would be more like it.' Then he added ironically, 'As for
being bored—that's amusing, coming from you. That word
applies to me.'

'Don't be ridiculous!' She spoke so emphatically that his
eyebrows lifted, but, ignoring his quizzical look, she went on
impatiently, 'You seem to have a thing about being a bore.
Of course I know that it originated with the story that Clare
invented. The one that broke up your—' she stopped as she
saw the grey eyes harden—'whatever it was with Fiona.'

He laughed grimly. 'Can't you find a word to describe it?
Well, I can. It was a love affair. I loved Fiona more, much
more than she loved me, but I didn't take that into account.
I fooled myself into imagining that when we were married
she would come to care equally for me. I know now that it
wouldn't have worked, but it hurt damnably at the time.
Now, however, I feel grateful to Clare for having saved me
from making a fool of myself.'

Longing to ask if he still loved Fiona, Joanna looked at
him searchingly, but the drawn expression on his face
seemed to warn her not to probe further. Instead she said,
'But you still have this fear of being thought a bore. That's
stupid when you know that Clare was lying.'

Paul shrugged. 'Maybe.' Then suddenly he laughed. 'It
seems that we've both been manipulated by other people.
I've learnt my lesson, however. Have you?'

Puzzled, Joanna said, 'I don't understand.'

'Don't you? Hasn't your experience made you wary of
falling in love again?'

Colour swept into her cheeks, but she said nothing and
after gazing at her long and thoughtfully, he nodded. 'Once
bitten, twice shy. Like me. Ah, well——' he glanced at his
watch and then looked round the room. 'Good lord, we're
the only ones left here! Let's go.'

For the rest of the journey back he spoke of Jenny, of
Lucky, of various incidents during the past week, and it
seemed to Joanna that he was already regretting their
intimate conversation. On arrival back at her flat she

asked him if he would like some tea, but he shook his head.

'No, thanks. I've got some letters to write.' Half mockingly he added, 'To Suffolk. I'm scouting around for a place in which to put up my plate. I've got my eyes on one or two houses, but so far it's all a bit vague. I'll have a good look round next weekend.' He paused. 'Now that you've decided not to have a puppy I don't suppose I shall see you there. Anyhow, have a nice time with your parents.' Suddenly, unexpectedly, he reached out and took her in his arms. Unable to resist, Joanna looked up at him steadily and saw that his eyes were sad. He said slowly, 'Will you miss me, Joanna, when I'm gone?'

She swallowed hard and turned her head away, fearful of betraying her longing for his kiss, but he turned her back to face him. His arms tightened round her and his voice trembled as he said, 'Do you think perhaps——?' He stopped abruptly, then slowly he added almost to himself, 'No. It's too much to ask. One of us will have to——' He stopped again and his eyes darkened as he muttered, 'God, you're so beautiful!' Bending his head, he kissed her with such passion that she almost cried out, then furiously she tried to pull herself away.'

'So beautiful,' she found the words echoing in her head. The usual reaction, she thought bitterly, ignoring the desolate look in Paul's eyes as he released her. 'Thank you for a lovely time,' she said calmly, and turning, went up to her flat, leaving him standing silently below.

That night she wept into her pillows. Paul wanted her that was obvious enough, but he didn't love her—the word had never passed his lips. If she had responded to him it would have meant repeating the fatal mistake she had made with James. Probably it would have gone even further, because her own desire for Paul was now so intense that it overshadowed all she had ever felt for James. That emotion was but a pale reflection of this all-consuming love she felt for a man who only wanted her physically. Desolately she faced the future. How would she ever be able to endure her life when Paul went away? It was said that time healed all things, but how long would it take for her to forget Paul? Probably she never would, for this love was the real thing. No other man could ever replace him in her heart.

CHAPTER NINE

THE WEEK that followed seemed to reflect Joanna's sadness. Surgeries were busy, but there were so many heartrending episodes that the consequent depression affected them all.

'Another Dead on Arrival.' Liz came out of the waiting room and said softly, 'Poor old lady. Her dog is obviously dead, but she won't believe it. Not only is it DOA but I think it's been dead since yesterday.'

'Oh, dear!' Joanna braced herself. 'Put the kettle on, please, Liz. A cup of tea might help her.'

The elderly lady came in slowly carrying a bundle wrapped in a shawl. Gradually unwinding it, she placed a little Yorkshire terrier on the table. Her face was drawn and pale and her voice shook as she said, 'I'm Mrs Greenwood and this is my darling Andy. I'm afraid he's very ill. Paralysed, I should think. I've had him fourteen years, but he's never acted so strangely before.' She paused and Joanna was about to speak, but she put up her hand. 'I must tell you what happened because you'll need to know all the symptoms. Yesterday morning he wouldn't get out of his basket, so thinking he was just tired I left him. Then he began making funny little noises, but that soon stopped and he went to sleep again. I left him there because when you're old you need a lot of rest. But later on in the day he went all stiff—he has a bit of rheumatism sometimes, so I let him stay. I offered him some food, but he simply ignored it.' She paused and laid her hand on the dog's coat. 'This morning the stiffness had all gone, but he's very cold and seems paralysed.'

Joanna swallowed hard and glanced at Liz, who began filling a mug with tea. Then, bending down, she began examining the little dog in order to satisfy Mrs

Greenwood. At last she looked up and said gently, 'I'm afraid it's bad news. Andy must have died yesterday morning. Those little noises he made—that was his heart giving up. The stiffness came on then, it always does after death——' She stopped as the old lady pulled herself erect and said angrily,

'Dead? Oh, no, that can't be true. You're only saying it because you don't know what's wrong.'

'Mrs Greenwood,' Joanna looked at her client in despair, 'I assure you—' she took her stethoscope and sounded the dog's heart once more, 'It's stopped. He's not breathing. He's been dead since yesterday.'

'But there was nothing wrong with him.' Mrs Greenwood wrung her hands. 'Give him an injection—see what you can do—don't just stand there!'

'There isn't any cure for old age.' Joanna was beginning to wonder if her client was going to have hysterics. 'Andy has had a long happy life and a very peaceful death. There really isn't anything I can do.'

Liz pulled up a chair and Mrs Greenwood sank on to it, staring ahead of her as though in a daze. When at last she spoke it was in a whisper. 'I know I'm old, but I've never seen death before.' She sipped mechanically at the tea Liz handed her, then getting up she went over to the still body on the table and stroked it, finally looking up at Joanna with tears streaming down her face. 'What shall I do now? I can't bury him. I haven't got a garden.'

'There's a very nice animal cemetary quite near here,' Joanna said carefully. 'If you like I'll make the necessary arrangements and then you can go and put flowers on his grave.'

It seemed to comfort Mrs Greenwood, and when at last she had gone Liz poured out more tea and the two girls sat drinking it in silence. Suddenly the telephone rang and Liz got up with a sigh of relief. 'Let's hope it's something more cheerful. We've had enough misery today. Ten cancers, cats to put to sleep—that little girl's hamster——' She picked up the receiver. 'Oh, hello, Paul. What? A monkey with a broken arm—yes, of course——' She handed the telephone to Joanna. 'He wants to speak to you.'

Joanna listened carefully as Paul explained, 'I'm at the zoo, but I can't put the arm in plaster here. The facilities are inadequate, so I'll have to bring it over. A little spot-nosed monkey. Will you have everything ready, please.'

'Well, that's something interesting,' Liz said cheerfully. 'I'm not very up on monkeys, are you, Joanna?'

Joanna laughed. 'I expect it will be pretty simple. After all, a broken limb on a monkey isn't all that different from a broken limb on any other animal.' She spoke calmly, but her heart was beating fast at Paul's imminent arrival. The mere mention of his name was enough to agitate her, and it took all her will power to disguise her feelings when he came into the surgery. He was accompanied by George the keeper who was carrying the monkey in a net.

'We had to catch him in this,' he said. 'Poor little devil was terrified. I never saw it happen—the accident to his arm, I mean—but he was probably cornered in a fight and got entangled in the bars of the cage.'

Joanna's heart contracted with pity at the look of terror in the brown eyes staring up at her. He was an attractive little monkey, distinguished by his peculiar marking—a heart-shaped blob of white fur on the very end of his nose. She bent down to try and soothe him, but he reared up frantically, chattering wildly. Paul said, 'I'll put the anaesthetic in his thigh,' and suiting the action to the word, he put the syringe through the net. A shriek of protest, then the chattering subsided and, as soon as the monkey was unconscious, George took off the net.

'Yes, it's broken,' Paul looked up from his

examination, 'here—on the lower end of the humerus—just above the elbow.' He turned to Liz. 'Water and plaster, please,' then he pulled the broken limb out straight, lined up the bones and set the arm. 'Joanna, will you hold it now? Keep up the tension while I put on the plaster. As you know, we must be quick or it will go hard.'

Beginning at the shoulder, he wound the plaster bandage right down the arm and the hand, covering the fingers, then wound it back up to the shoulder again. A little more manipulation of the bones before the plaster hardened, an injection of antibiotic and, at last, he stood back satisfied.

'How long will he have to keep it on?' asked George.

'Three weeks, and he'll have to be isolated for that time. When I take the plaster off that's when your problems will begin.'

George looked rueful. 'Yes. We'll have to find somewhere else for him to live. Probably with a different species. His present companions won't accept him back and we can't risk any more fights.'

'I'll be in tomorrow to see how he is,' Paul said as George took the monkey in his arms and, as the door shut behind him, Liz said,

'A coffee? Have you time?'

He nodded, 'Very welcome,' then turning to Joanna he said, 'Why do you look so serious? Don't you like monkeys?'

'It's not that. I pity them and I hate the idea of that poor little creature and all the others kept in captivity. It confirms my dislike of zoos.'

'I agree with you.' He gazed thoughtfully into the mug of coffee in his hand. 'Those monkeys are not even an endangered species. There's really no excuse for keeping them in cages, however large. It hurts me to look into their eyes—they surely must yearn for freedom.'

'Oh, dear!' Liz said sympathetically. 'There's so much

sadness in the animal world. Sometimes it makes me feel quite sick to think of what goes on, and it's even worse in other parts of the world. There are some countries where they don't give a damn about animals' feelings. Donkeys like Jenny beaten and half-starved—dogs reared to be eaten——' Suddenly her eyes filled with tears and she took refuge in the dispensary.

Seeing the look of pity in Paul's eyes, Joanna felt that she herself could easily give way to tears. When Paul showed the sensitive side of his nature all her love for him came to the fore. If only—— Blindly she turned away to hide her feelings, then suddenly she stiffened as his arms enfolded her. Immediately he released her. 'Sorry,' his voice was cold, 'I was merely trying to comfort you, but you obviously don't like me touching you.' He turned on his heel and went out silently, leaving Joanna with the feeling that her whole world was falling apart. Everything she said or did was misunderstood. His touch—why, it set her alight with love for him! If he only knew how she longed for that love to be returned! Fighting hard to overcome her sadness, she told herself sternly not to give way to self-pity and was thankful to be distracted by the sound of the telephone. Lifting the receiver, she heard Andrew's voice.

'I'm off duty this evening. Will you come out to dinner with me?' he asked, and added pleadingly, 'Please don't say no. I've had a hell of a day—very lowering. I need cheering up.'

Joanna hesitated. 'I don't know. I've had a beastly day too. I thought I'd have an early night.'

'You've got it wrong. An evening out is the best cure for depression. Say yes.'

She pondered for a moment, then decided. He was right. What was the use of letting her thoughts dwell on Paul? She must learn to live her life without him.

He sounded so delighted when she agreed that she

smiled as she put down the receiver, then suddenly she frowned. A quick look at the roster and she realised she had been too impulsive.

Liz looked at her curiously as she came out of the dispensary. 'What's wrong?'

'I've accepted an invitation to go out tonight, but I shouldn't have. I'm on duty.'

Liz shrugged and laughed. 'I wouldn't let that stand in my way if I were you. You've done more than your fair share of being on call. In any case, Freddy will stand in for you. He's always willing. I think he likes small animal work better than large. I'll contact him for you.'

'Only too pleased,' Freddy said when he came on the line. 'I'll do the evening surgery too if you like.'

Resolutely closing her mind to Paul, Joanna spent a long time over her appearance and when she went down to greet Andrew he stood for a moment gazing at her in admiration.

'You look so lovely with your hair down like that, and that dress—oh, I know you've worn it before, but if I had my way you'd wear it all the time.' He grinned. 'That's a pretty silly thing to say, but whenever I see you I'm knocked sideways.' He shut the car door, then turned to glance at her. 'A bad day, was it? Like mine, I expect.'

'Well, I don't suppose it compares with yours,' she said thoughtfully. 'It can't be easy for you to shake off human tragedies.'

He put his hand on her knee before changing gear. 'You'd make a marvellous doctor's wife, Joanna. If only—' he frowned, 'well, I can't help hoping that one day you'll change your mind.'

She sat in silence pondering his words as they drove out into the countryside, and as she listened to Andrew's description of his day her heart warmed towards him. He was so kind that she began to wonder if she ought to take him more seriously. Turning the idea over in her mind, she tried to ignore the knowledge that Andrew could never arouse the deep, passionate love that she felt for Paul. Desperately she tried to obliterate all thoughts of him and did her best to be a cheerful companion. Listening to Andrew's problems, laughing at his jokes even though to her own ears her laughter sounded a little forced, she wondered guiltily if she was raising false hopes in him. Throughout the evening she was at her most animated, showing great interest in his plans for the future and taking obvious pleasure in the delicious food and drink he chose from the extensive menu. At last, rather carried away, she said,

'I never realised before what a fascinating life a doctor has or—' she smiled at him teasingly, 'how fascinating the doctor himself could be. I expect your lady patients——' She stopped abruptly as his eyes narrowed.

Leaning forward, he gazed at her steadily. 'Joanna, you're putting on an act. Why?'

The direct question stunned her. Her cheeks turned scarlet and she looked down at the table. Struggling for words, she could find no answer, and glancing up at last, she met his gaze with her own eyes full of regret.

Andrew's mouth twisted as he saw her confusion, then he said evenly, 'You're trying too hard. I appreciate your efforts to make the evening enjoyable, but I can't for one moment believe that you find me—er—fascinating.'

Her high colour faded and she became very pale. Ashamed, she looked away for a moment, then said simply, 'I'm sorry, Andrew.'

His smile was tinged with bitterness. 'OK, but what are you trying to prove? That it's as easy to love one man as another?'

Shaken at his perspicacity, she nodded. 'That's about it. Silly of me.'

'Rather cruel, I think,' he said coolly. 'Cut it out, please. I know very well that you're in love with Paul, but one thing puzzles me. I would have taken a bet that he's in love with you, so what makes you so unhappy? What's wrong?'

Joanna evaded the question and questioned the statement. 'Paul isn't in love with me. What makes you think he is?'

'Well, he's a fool if he isn't,' Andrew said sharply, 'a beautiful girl like you.'

He had touched on a sore point, and she reacted accordingly.

'Beauty,' she said contemptuously, 'that's all that counts with men, isn't it?'

'Rubbish!' he said scornfully. 'Beauty attracts men, of course if does, but when it comes to love it's personality and character that really matter. Look around you—plenty of plain girls and equally plain men make happy couples. I'm sure that Paul——' he stopped, heaved a long sigh, then gave a short laugh. 'I can't think why I'm pleading his case, except that I don't like to see you unhappy.'

'Well, I'm endeavouring to get the better of that,' Joanna said firmly. 'That's why——'

Andrew smiled grimly. 'That's why you've come out with me.' He paused. 'If I thought I had the slightest chance with you I'd jump at it. But I haven't, have I?'

She looked at him wistfully. If only she could get Paul out of her system—would it then be possible to be happy with Andrew? A good, kind steady friend—rather like a brother. But one didn't marry one's brother, and marriage was what was in Andrew's mind.

'You haven't answered my question,' his voice broke in on her reflections. 'What are you thinking?'

She looked up. 'That I look upon you as a nice brother,' she said frankly, and seeing his mouth drop she knew she had again put paid to his hopes.

He took it well, made light conversation as they drove

back, but as they stood in the surgery yard, he said quietly,

'One kiss, please, Joanna. One kiss to last me for a long, long time, if not for ever.' He smiled a little grimly. 'I realise that I shall probably recover, but please, one last kiss, and not—' he hesitated, 'not a brotherly one.'

Clasped in his arms, Joanna assented willingly. Reaching up, she stroked the back of his head and tried to respond to the passion he made no attempt to control. At last she could take no more and was on the point of trying to push him away when there was a sudden blinding surge of headlights and a car came through the open gates into the yard. For a moment Andrew continued to hold her, then with a muttered, 'Goodbye, my love,' he went swiftly to his car. As he drove down to the bottom of the yard in order to turn Joanna recognised Paul sitting at the wheel waiting for Andrew to pass him and, horrified, she fled up to her flat. Without turning on the light she went to the window and watched the cars manoeuvring carefully, and as Andrew passed through the gates, she saw Paul get out. A minute later the light was switched on in the surgery. Wondering if she ought to go down and help in a possible emergency, she hesitated, then determined to wait until she was asked. But five minutes later the light went out and Paul returned to his car. Breathing a heartfelt sigh of relief, she watched him drive away and at last she switched on the light in her flat.

Over a large cup of coffee, she gave herself up to bitter, regretful thoughts. It seemed that at every turn she was being brought face to face with a fresh problem. As soon as her association with Paul became reasonably tolerable something disastrous occurred to set them at odds again. What he would make of the scene shown up in his headlights she could only imagine. Perhaps it would make very little impression and would only confirm him in his fixed conviction that she loved Andrew. Well, there was nothing she could do about it—nothing at all.

Next morning in the surgery she tried not to let her personal affairs detract from her usual competence. Work, she decided, was the only way in which to forget her troubles, and there was plenty of that. It was a morning of gratifying successes. Patients came in to have their sutures taken out, grateful owners were pleased that operations had been successful, children's faces lit up when their pets' ailments were shown to be curable, no animals had to be put to sleep and there were no argumentative clients.

'A lovely morning,' said Liz as surgery ended, 'and now you've got a nice trip out to the country this afternoon. Mr Osborne lives in one of the cottages just by Claytons' Farm. It's his springer spaniel you're going to see. Will you have coffee here or are you going over to see Mrs Holman?'

The thought of Mrs Holman's kindly curiosity held no appeal to Joanna in her present frame of mind and she settled down with Liz at the surgery table. Then, suddenly, the outside door slammed and Paul came in, limping rather badly. 'Kicked by a stallion,' he said briefly, and went into the dispensary. Joanna and Liz glanced at each other, then followed him in. Paul had his leg up on a stool and was rubbing ointment into his knee.

'It's not cracked, is it?' Joanna asked anxiously, and he shook his head as he pulled down his trouser leg.

'No, thank goodness. A bit painful, that's all. I was lucky to get away with only a kick. Mr Harwood, the owner, had his face bitten and has had to go to hospital. It was his own fault, actually. He went into the stable when the stallion was eating his hay, tripped over something, and the sudden movement alarmed the horse who turned wildly and caught him with his teeth. Mr Harwood tried to defend himself but fell on the ground, and I had to drag him away before he was trampled on.'

He came out of the dispensary and grinned wryly as he saw the cup of tea Liz immediately put in front of him. 'Treating me for shock? Well, it's all in the day's work. But it's a pity about Mr Harwood. He's devoted to that stallion—drives him about in a gig. He would never let the animal be castrated, but he'll have to now, of course. That will be some job. I'll have to get Mark or Freddy to help me with the anaesthetising.'

'Oh, I'd like to see that,' Liz said impulsively, then stopped at the sight of Joanna's face.

'No, you wouldn't,' Joanna said briefly, and Paul's mouth twitched at the corner.

'You wouldn't be welcome,' he said. 'Mr Harwood would be embarrassed—like a lot of farmers, he's rather puritanical.'

'That's ridiculous,' Liz said hotly. 'We castrate dogs and cats—what a Victorian attitude!'

'Maybe,' Paul grinned sardonically, 'but in this case, I agree with the farmer.'

'Old-fashioned, that's what you are,' said Liz indignantly, and took herself off to the office, leaving Joanna alone with Paul. This was the last thing she wanted, so, hurriedly emptying her mug of coffee, she rose to her feet.

'Tea but no sympathy,' he said drily. 'I expect if I were Andrew you would be consoling me with ardent kisses.' He smiled cynically as her cheeks flamed. 'That was a very romantic scene I witnessed last night. I'm sorry I broke it up. You seemed to be enjoying it.'

Her mouth trembled but she said sharply, 'It was a farewell kiss.'

He laughed, a harsh, mocking sound that hurt her even more than the scornful look in his eyes. 'Really? Well, in that case can I count on the same token of affection when I leave here?'

Angrily she turned away and he said grimly, 'On second thoughts I expect I'll have to be content with a handshake. I obviously don't come into the same category as Andrew.'

In the dispensary Joanna stood, hands clenched in anger at the fresh blow dealt her by Fate, then to her relief she heard the door shut as Paul went out to his car.

Driving out to the country that afternoon, Joanna concentrated on the beauty of the autumn colours. Leaves were slowly falling from the trees, but it was unusually warm with a brilliant blue sky. It was soothing and therapeutic even though there was a hint of melancholy in the fact that soon the trees would be bare and cold winds would usher in winter. Rather like a picture of her own future, Joanna thought pensively. She must take comfort in the knowledge that her work demanded great concentration and would, she hoped fervently, help to deaden her heartache when Paul had gone. It had aided her in recovering from the searing disillusionment she had experienced after James's death, so perhaps work and time would soften this second hard blow, although the feelings she had had for James were pale and ephemeral compared with the deep love she had for Paul. Suddenly realising that she was sliding back into depression, she gave herself a mental shake. She must live in the present and make the best of it.

Slowing down as she passed the Claytons' farm, she pulled up at the gate of the first of three cottages a few yards further on. An elderly man stood outside and, knowing what she had to do, Joanna felt her heart sink.

'Hello, Mr Osborne,' she smiled at him, 'I'm Joanna Bramford. I've replaced Jean Russell.'

He nodded slowly. 'I know. Mrs Clayton has told me all about you. Come inside.'

He led her up the path, then hesitated at the door. 'It's a sad business, miss, but I've been through it many times before. My old Bess can't go on any longer. She's nearly fifteen years old.'

The old springer spaniel lay in her comfortable bed, and although her tail lifted in recognition as her master approached there was a mournful weariness in her greeting that made a lump come into Joanna's throat.

Mr Osborne said quietly, 'I'll talk to her for a moment, then—' he swallowed painfully—'as quickly and mercifully as possible, please.'

Joanna turned her back, opened her case and filled a syringe. Waiting quietly, she saw the old man go on his knees and put his arm round Bess, who looked up, her dim eyes full of love. 'My good old girl,' he said brokenly, then suddenly, buoyantly he said, 'Missus—yes, you're going to see your missus.' Signing to Joanna, he repeated it, and Bess's tail wagged in joyful understanding as the needle slipped in. Tears ran down Joanna's cheeks as she pulled herself erect and as Bess slipped into unconsciousness Mr Osborne rose to his feet. The final lethal injection given, he said, 'Come along now, miss. You need a cup of tea and so do I.'

Seated at the table, she watched as he moved about briskly and when at last he sat down opposite her she asked quietly, 'When did you lose your wife?'

He sighed. 'Six months ago. She went suddenly, and Bess has pined for her ever since. Well,' he paused, 'she's happy now, but I've got to go on. Perhaps you think I'm just a foolish old man, but I feel sure that we'll all meet again—Doris and I and all our dogs.' He looked up, his eyes moist. 'Why not? We're supposed to be going to perfect happiness with our loved ones, and as we've never had any children, our loved ones were our dogs.'

Joanna nodded in full agreement. 'Why not indeed? What will you do now? Another dog?'

'Oh, yes. I couldn't live without one. I'm still fit enough—walk five miles a day, do my house and garden—I can still give a dog a good life, and a dog will give me something to live for.'

Joanna nodded again. The companionship of old

people and animals was something she understood well. She asked gently, 'Have you another dog in mind?'

'Oh, yes, I'm very lucky there. Mr Copeland, he often drops in to see me when he's called to the Claytons' farm—he's going to give me one. A litter from his sister's bitch. All the way from Suffolk.' His sad face lit up at last. 'He's giving it to me, and you know what a dog like that costs.'

Joanna, brought up short at the mention of Paul's name, sat for a minute in astonished silence. A surge of love swept over her for the outwardly hard and cynical man who was in reality so generous and kind.

'There's no one like him,' Mr Osborne's quiet observation put her thoughts into words. 'I've known him for several years. Many's the time he's sat here with me and my missus. I used to work on Mr Clayton's farm and when I retired he made a point of dropping in to see us.'

When Joanna rose to leave he said quietly, 'No need to take Bess with you. I'm going to bury her in the garden.' He followed her to the gate, then, just as she was getting into her car, he called suddenly, 'Wait a minute, there's Mr Clayton—he's beckoning to you.'

The farmer looked agitated. 'I've been trying to get Mr Copeland. I don't know what's got into you all at the surgery. I've rung several times, but your girl says she's having difficulty in contacting him. I've got a calving on my hands that I can't cope with myself and it's getting urgent.' He frowned. 'Do you think you could help? I know I made a few jokes about women vets, but you did say you'd all received the same training, so——'

Joanna tried to hide the sudden nervousness that swept over her. 'Of course I'll help,' she said briskly, then on a sudden thought she added, 'I haven't got a parturition gown with me. Could you lend me something?'

'Well, I can find an overall—might be a bit long, but you can hitch it up.' He opened the farm gate and led the way towards the calving box. Handing her a vast overall, he seemed suddenly smitten with doubt as she went up to the big black and white Friesian cow standing tied up to a ring in the wall. 'I don't know that I ought to have asked you. She's one of our best milkers and I don't want to lose her or the calf.'

Joanna said nothing and began calmly to examine the cow. Standing back reluctantly, Mr Clayton watched her in silence, and at last she said quietly, 'The front leg is turned back on itself. I must get hold of the hoof in order to pull it forward.'

It was not as easy as it sounded and when, finally, she found what she was seeking, the hoof was so far back that she could only just reach it with the tips of her fingers. All her strength was needed to hold on as the cow gave a strong contraction and, for a few minutes, she felt despairingly that the job was beyond her physical capability. Grimly she persevered in spite of the painful bruising of her arm, then suddenly, in between two contractions, she managed at last to straighten out the leg. After that, it was comparatively simple. Mr Clayton handed her the ropes which she tied with a slip knot round the calf's protruding head and they waited for the next contraction. Two strong pulls and she gasped with delight as the calf fell on to the straw.

For a moment she felt dazed, then, flushed with success, she stood back and watched as Mr Clayton took off the ropes, unhooked the cow from the ring on the wall and gently dragged the calf up to its mother. Hesitatingly, almost doubtfully, she gave it a little nudge, then, with a soft moo of pleasure, she began to lick it all over with her rough tongue.

'A fine little heifer,' a deep voice from behind Joanna made her jump wildly and turning swiftly she saw Paul standing in the entrance to the box. Her heart hammering, she sat down quickly on a bale of hay.

Mr Clayton laughed. 'Well, what do you know? A

woman vet is as good as a man. What do you say to that, Mr Copeland?'

Paul laughed, his eyes on Joanna. 'You're the one who had the doubts, if you remember. It's no more than I would expect.'

Then, as Mr Clayton went over to inspect the calf, Paul asked quietly, 'Are you OK, Joanna? You look all in.'

Unable to tell him that it was his unexpected arrival that had caused her sudden weakness, she got up from the hay bale. 'I'm all right, thank you, but I must admit that if it had been more complicated I might have found it a bit too much for me.'

'Fair enough,' he assented amiably. 'Still it's very satisfying for you to have succeeded in what's never an easy job.' He turned as Mr Clayton came up.

'A cup of tea—oh, yes, you must. My wife will be pleased to hear the good news.'

When at last they left the farm, Paul looked at Joanna searchingly. 'Are you sure you're not too tired to drive? I know your arm must be badly bruised. You can come back in my car if you like and later on we can drive over to collect yours.'

Pleased at his concern but knowing it was unnecessary, she thanked him but refused, and drove away leaving him looking doubtful. It was silly of her, she reflected, to have been so shaken up by his unexpected arrival. Sighing, she thought of his pleasant concern and his generous praise. What a complex relationship theirs was! Rather like living on the edge of a minefield—one false step and then a deadly explosion. Perhaps that was an indication that there were hidden depths on both sides. On Paul's part, however, she was convinced that it was merely physical desire that he felt for her, and that was not enough. Not for her anyway. Then, suddenly, a thought struck her that was like a flash of lightning. Instinctively she slowed down and pulled into the side of the road as she considered it. Suppose she went along with him? Suppose she let him know that she was also attracted to him in that way?—which was, of course, perfectly true. Would an affair with him lead him eventually to falling in love with her?

She was so deep in thought that she failed to notice that a car had drawn up behind her. Then, with a start, she saw Paul looking in at her through the open window.

'I knew you weren't feeling too good,' he said accusingly. 'Look, lock up your car and leave it here. I'll drive you back.'

'No, you're quite mistaken,' she shook her head as he opened her car door. 'I'm perfectly all right.'

He gave a puzzled frown. 'Why did you stop here, then?'

Wondering wryly what he would say if she told him, she said untruthfully, 'I needed a quiet think. I was worrying about going home for the weekend.' She saw the incredulous look in his eyes and added impulsively, 'Whenever I ring my mother she reproaches me for having left it so long, but I dread returning to Suffolk.'

'Good lord!' He stared at her. 'That's stretching it a bit far, isn't it?'

'You don't understand,' she said sharply, and put her hand on the ignition key. 'Anyway, there's no need for you to drive me back.'

Paul drew back, rebuffed, and immediately penitent, she said, 'Thank you all the same. It was kind of you.'

Looking in her mirror as she drove away she saw him standing looking after her and felt an overwhelming desire to burst into tears. What a fool she was! According to her new plan she should have let him drive her back and accepted his comfort and sympathy. Then gradually she stopped reproaching herself. She couldn't play that game. It was not in her character, and the idea of leading him into an affair which would be loveless on his part suddenly appalled her. She must let him go away without knowing that she loved him. A clean break when it came.

Then—what then? Joanna shrugged to herself. Life could not deal her any worse blow than saying goodbye to him. Beyond that, the future was dark.

CHAPTER TEN

THE MEETING at the Mayfields house bore out everything Paul had forecast. Radical changes were shown to be necessary and Joanna, listening carefully, was forced to agree that this modernisation was well planned and would lead to a better organised and very efficient practice. Expansion too was inevitable, as Mr Mayfield explained, and although he himself had never been keen on the idea of branch practices that must also be given serious consideration.

Later, in the general discussion that followed, Joanna found herself talking to Freddy Conway, and it emerged from his conversation that he was one of the prime instigators of the need for change. 'It's the only way nowadays,' he said. 'Competition in the profession is becoming as fierce as it is in the business world. This practice can't afford to rest on its laurels.'

'That's as maybe,' suddenly Joanna realised that Paul had come up behind her, 'but this building of empires does tend to do away with the personal relationship between a vet and his clients. I agree that one must be up to date with regard to all the latest developments in scientific information and surgical equipment, but fear of competition is a money-based motive.' He paused and frowned. 'Surely money is not the objective where the care of animals is concerned. We must live, of course, and be paid enough to justify our training and knowledge, but to go all out for profit in the business sense—' he shook his head firmly—'That's not my scene at all.'

Freddy shrugged. 'Very laudable, but don't you think it's a shade too idealistic?'

Joanna cut in sharply. 'I don't. I agree with Paul. What's wrong with being idealistic anyway? That's

174

what the veterinary profession is all about—care and compassion for our patients and a desire to improve their lot. This often means long discussions with their owners, and that takes time. The business world says time is money, but in our work money should be a secondary consideration.'

Freddy grinned broadly as he glanced from one to the other. 'What a starry-eyed couple you are! You should set up together in some small town and give all your services free.'

Paul laughed. 'That would be most unethical. All the other local vets would go broke.'

Freddy laughed mockingly as he moved away and after a moment's silence, Paul said, 'It's an idea, though.'

'What is?' Joanna looked amused, 'working for nothing?'

'No,' he gazed at her steadily, 'but what about setting up together.'

For an instant she was dazzled at the picture he conjured up in her imagination and, seeing the light in her eyes, Paul was about to continue when her expression changed and she shook her head.

'I don't think your ideas would coincide with mine,' she said. 'Your dream of a practice in Suffolk is my idea of a nightmare!' She managed a stiff little smile and turned away. But it was not easy to forget his astonishing suggestion. It stayed in her mind, tormenting her far into the night. At last, as she lay sleepless in bed, she rejected the whole idea. Working with Paul would undoubtedly be easy—professionally they were in accord—but it would be nothing short of torture if, as time passed, he met and fell in love with someone and got married. That was a possibility that made her go cold all over, but it could not be ignored. And always there was the unacceptable fact that Paul was fixed on working in Suffolk and that, to her, was quite out of the question. She had been right to turn his offer down, and by now, having realised that he had spoken too impulsively, he must be thinking the same.

Saturday morning she set out very early and, inevitably as she drove towards her parents' home, her thoughts turned to the time when she had made the journey in reverse. She had been so glad to get away—so sure that she was doing the right thing. Now, as she passed familiar landmarks, she began to question her wisdom in not staying to face up to the malicious gossip that she had found so hurtful. All she had achieved was unhappiness of a different kind—one over which she had no control whatsoever. In an endeavour to escape from such troubled thoughts she flooded the car with music and the Beethoven Pastoral Symphony put a temporary end to her doubts and fears.

The drive was long but uneventful, and seeing the joy in her parents' faces she made a resolution to visit them more often. To be sure, she had felt a pang of regret as she drove through the village where Mr Bridges had his practice, and as it was only two miles from her parents' home she promised herself that she would drop in to see him before going back. This idea was confirmed when, at lunch, her father said; 'I saw poor old Bridges the other day and told him you were coming down. Why don't you go in to see him this afternoon?'

'That's a good idea,' Mrs Bramford said cheerfully. 'We could do some shopping first, then I'll drop you off at the surgery, continue my shopping and pick you up on my way back.'

'I'd like that,' Joanna smiled, 'but, Dad, why did you say "poor" old Bridges?'

Her father frowned. 'Well, I don't know really. Perhaps it was that he looked so down in the dumps. He had to get rid of that assistant who took your place, hasn't yet found another and is working far too hard for a man of his age.'

'Well, I expect he'll find someone eventually,' said Mrs Bramford quickly. 'No need for you to look so remorseful, Joanna. I'm sure you did the right thing in going away—not because of the gossip, that's all died down—but you needed a change and the experience of a larger practice.'

It was when Joanna and her mother were going round the one department store in the little town that she realised the truth of her mother's statement. They met several acquaintances who greeted her in such a friendly way that she began to wonder if she had overreacted to the criticism that had forced her to leave the district. Over tea and cakes she put the question to her mother.

Mrs Bramford nodded thoughtfully. 'People are funny, you know. Soon after you left they seemed to go over to your side, especially the animal owners who couldn't get on with Mr Bridges' assistant. And I did a bit of work on your behalf as well. Telling them the whole truth—ramming it home forcibly that you never knew James was married.' She hesitated. 'You're not sorry you left, are you? I don't want to pry, but sometimes when we've been talking on the telephone it's struck me that you were a bit tense.'

Anxious to put her mother's mind at rest, Joanna said lightly, 'Well, it was a bit strange at first, a completely new way of life for me, and it took a little time to get adjusted. But I've settled in now and find it very interesting.' She glanced at her watch. 'I'll tell you and Dad more about my job this evening, but I'd better go and see Mr Bridges now before he begins his evening surgery.'

He was delighted to see her, but she was distressed at his appearance. He seemed to have aged so much since the comparatively short time she had been away that she wondered if he was ill, and seeing her ill-disguised concern, he nodded casually.

'I know what you're thinking, and you're right. I've been overdoing things and, in fact, my doctor has given me some advice that I find hard to take but know I must accept. I'm going to sell this practice.'

Astonished, Joanna stared at him and her eyes grew even wider as he continued, 'I've already got a young vet interested in buying it—he's coming to see me soon, should be here any time now. No, don't go, my dear—' he put out his hand as Joanna half rose from her chair, 'he's a colleague of yours in Sussex. A Mr Copeland.'

Thunderstruck, Joanna was silent for a long minute. Then, collecting her wits, she asked, 'How did he come to hear of it?'

'Ah,' Mr Bridges laughed, 'that's a giveaway! You obviously don't read your *Veterinary Record*. Well, not the practices for sale advertisements, anyway. I put the ad in last week and Mr Copeland was the first to answer it. He rang me at once and said it was just what he was looking for. Seemed a very nice chap. Is he?'

'Oh, yes. He comes from this part of the world and is dead keen to return. I should think this practice is ideal for him.' Joanna paused. 'All the same, I think I'd better go now. You'll want to talk business.'

But it was too late. The sound of a car pulling up outside got Mr Bridges to his feet and, as he went to the door, he said, 'Hold on a minute. I want to show you something.'

Longing to escape, Joanna was forced to remain and, drawing a deep breath, she tried to calm her fast beating heart. Telling herself that there was no reason why she should not be here and no reason at all why she should avoid meeting Paul, she managed to get herself in hand, greeting him calmly when Mr Bridges brought him into the room.'

'Good lord—Joanna!' He stared at her in amazement. 'Don't tell me you're thinking of buying this practice after all you've said about Suffolk?'

Before she could answer, Mr Bridges laughed. 'If that were the case she would have the first refusal, but I don't think——' He paused. 'As I said just now—I've got something to show you. Excuse me a minute. I shan't be long.'

As he went into his office Paul said, 'I expect you're surprised to see me here, but when I saw the advertisement in the *Veterinary Record* I changed my idea at once about putting up my plate. An old-established practice like this would be marvellous. I don't know yet what Mr Bridges is asking, but I shall do my damnedest to raise the necessary.'

Joanna smiled wryly at the sight of his enthusiasm. Somehow the thought of Paul working in the surroundings where she herself had been so happy moved her in a way she could not quite understand. Was it envy, she wondered, or was it just sadness at the thought of his leaving Sussex? Before she had time to work it out Mr Bridges came back and handed her a book which she recognised as his desk diary. Handing it over, he said, 'Look at this carefully, beginning at the week after you left here. You'll see some pencilled remarks against certain clients that should interest you. Study it while Mr Copeland and I talk business in the office.'

Left alone, Joanna wondered for a moment if her ex-employer was turning strange in his old age. What on earth had this diary to do with her? Puzzled, she opened the book, and as she turned the pages it gradually became clear.

Here and there a name she remembered stood out, and in the margin alongside, Mr Bridges had made cryptic remarks. 'Mrs Hebben—put her right about Joanna. Told her to pass it on. Mrs Wharton—unwilling to believe me at first but convinced at last. Mr Burrell——' So it went on, and recalling that these clients had been among the ones who had been so cold towards her, Joanna shut the book at last and stared ahead, marvelling at the old man's kindness. What with his help and her mother's efforts her name was cleared, and that accounted for the friendly atmosphere she had

encountered in town this afternoon. Blinking hard to hold
back tears of gratitude, she went to the window to see if
her mother's car was approaching. For some minutes she
stood there, hearing subconsciously the low hum of voices
from the office, and suddenly the door opened and Mr
Bridges came out, followed by Paul. From the look in his
eyes Joanna could see that all had gone satisfactorily, and
Mr Bridges said, 'If there's anything else you need to
know just give me a ring. I won't see anyone else until
you've decided.'

As the two men shook hands Joanna heard the bell ring
and turning to her old employer she reached up and gave
him a grateful kiss. His face lit up as she said softly, 'that
was such a kind thing to do. Thank you very, very much.'
Handing back the diary just as her mother came in, she
introduced Paul hurriedly, hoping to get away before he
asked any curious questions. As she and her mother went
towards the door she realised that Paul was following
them after having just said goodbye to Mr Bridges. He
came up just as she was getting into the car beside her
mother.'

'Joanna, do you think you could spare me a little
time this weekend? Mr Bridges would like my decision
before I go back and I'd rather like to talk it over with
you.'

Before she could answer her mother said, 'Come to
lunch, Mr Copeland,' and proceeded to give the address,
while Joanna, half angry, half amused, could not find it in
her heart to rebuke her mother for taking matters so
firmly in her own hands. But why, she asked herself, did
Paul want to discuss his personal affairs with her? In the
preceding week he had not made any mention of having
contacted Mr Bridges, though that was probably due to
lack of opportunity. Surely he had no doubts about the
practice? Mr Bridges had nothing to hide and it was quite
plainly what Paul wanted. Unable to solve the problem,
Joanna put it aside and gave herself up to entertaining

her parents with tales of her work.

She awoke early on Sunday morning and going to the open window she drew in long breaths of the invigorating air. Suddenly she found herself half regretting that she must leave here so soon. She must, she decided, return more often. It would please her parents and she herself would benefit from the break. And, of course, see Paul occasionally. No—she frowned—that would be foolish. She would be turning the knife in her wounded heart. That was not the way to forget him, and forget him she must if she were ever going to be able to recover her peace of mind.

He arrived promptly and very quickly became engrossed in conversation with her parents. Surreptitiously she glanced at him now and then, thinking how handsome and strong he looked, how his eyes lit up with animation as he talked of his love for this part of the world, and her heart sank at the thought of working so far away from him. Suddenly she met her mother's eyes and saw that her face had betrayed her. Hurriedly she went into the kitchen under the pretence of seeing how the meal was progressing, but to her consternation her mother followed, looking extremely thoughtful.

'I like that young man very much, Joanna. Do you?' The question hung on the air as Joanna felt her colour rising. Then, to cover up her feelings, she said a little irritably,

'He's all right, a good vet. We get on professionally, but we fight a lot when it comes to personal matters.''

'Personal matters? What do you mean?' Mrs Bramford looked puzzled.

'Oh, nothing. I can't explain. Look out—that saucepan is about to boil over!'

Relieved at having distracted her mother, Joanna went back into the living room and as Paul rose to his feet he said, 'I've been telling your father about the litter of springer spaniels over at my sister's house. He's very interested and suggests that you should come with me after lunch to look at them with a view to choosing one.'

Surprised and reluctant to be alone with Paul, she said, 'Won't you come as well, Dad?'

Her father laughed. 'I'm quite content to leave it to you vets. In any case, I like my nap after lunch.'

Her mother, when asked, also declined on the grounds that she always tended to choose the runt of a litter out of pity for its weakness and Joanna, despite her misgivings, forced herself to look cheerful until the meal was over. Then she said, 'I thought you wanted to talk to me about buying Mr Bridges' practice, Paul, though I can't really see why you should want my advice.'

'But I do,' he said quietly, 'so let's see the dogs first, then we can go for a drive and talk.'

Paul's sister proved to be so friendly that Joanna warmed to her in spite of her original doubts, and she and her large easygoing husband were obviously very fond of Paul.

'We're so pleased that he's thinking of settling down in this area,' Jane Rogers confided as they went out to the warm stable where the puppies and their mother were temporarily installed. 'All he needs now is a wife——' She sighed. 'I expect you've heard about that business with Fiona. We never quite knew what went wrong, but it took him a long time to get over it.'

Fortunately Joanna was spared from making any comment as they had now reached the stable, and soon they were gazing down at the beautiful puppies stumbling about over their magnificent mother.

'They're fantastic!' Joanna exclaimed. 'They're all so strong and healthy-looking. How on earth can we choose?'

Paul bent down and studied them closely. 'That one there—look, he's obviously the leader—a tough little fellow.' He picked up a puppy with well defined liver and white markings, a plump little body and large white paws. 'Your father said he and your mother wanted a big dog—those paws are a good indication. What do you think?'

He handed it to her and she examined it closely, then nodded in agreement. 'He's perfect,' she said.

Paul's sister laughed. 'I might have known it! You've chosen the pick of the litter. He's going to be a very handsome dog.'

Paul said, 'Now I want one for an old friend. That pretty little bitch over there. Just the job. When they're ready to leave their mother I'll come over again and take that one back with me.'

When at last they had left the rambling old house Joanna felt more at ease. The friendly reception, the relaxing fun with the puppies, all had combined to make a most enjoyable outing.

Paul glanced at her glowing face as they got into his car. 'My sister liked you very much,' he said. 'She's a very good judge of character too.'

Joanna laughed. 'Nice of her, but she hasn't seen me when I'm in a temper.' She paused, then added drily, 'When you and I are fighting, for instance.'

'Oh, she knows about the rows we have,' he said easily. 'She thinks it's a good sign.'

Joanna turned to stare at him. 'What on earth——? A good sign of what?' Resentful at having been talked over by brother and sister, she showed her displeasure openly and added sharply, 'You needn't answer that. I don't want to know.'

He said smoothly, 'Sorry if I upset you, but my sister and I have always been great friends, and she's interested in my future.'

'I can't see——' Joanna began, then stopped. At all costs she must prevent another quarrel, but Paul persisted.

'You can't see what my future has to do with you? Is that what you were going to say?'

'Yes,' she said briefly, then suddenly as she stared ahead she felt a twinge of anxiety. 'You're driving towards the coast! Oh, Paul, I'd rather not go there.'

'You're just being foolish,' he said sternly. 'It's a good time of the year for a walk along the beach. No one there.'

'Please—I couldn't bear it!' Even to her own ears Joanna's voice sounded almost hysterical, and glancing at her quickly, Paul laid his hand gently on her knee.

'All right. No need to get so upset,' he said soothingly. 'We'll stop up there—in that opening off the lane. I want to ask you something.'

Calmer now, she waited in silence until he spoke again.

'This practice of Mr Bridges—I've already made up my mind to buy it, but what I want to know is whether you would care to come in with me as a partner. No, don't shake your head like that—listen. Mr Bridges is moving out, the house is very nice—huge garden, lots of room. He's asking very much less than I expected, which would leave me enough to take in a partner straight away. You wouldn't have to put in any capital. I'd live in the house and you could either live with your parents or in a flat somewhere in the vicinity. How about it?'

It was such a generous offer that Joanna was left speechless, almost in a state of shock.

'Stunned you, have I?' Paul asked drily. 'Oh, I know there are obstacles in the way. Your dislike of Suffolk—well, you're not the neurotic type and I'm sure you would eventually overcome that. The sea so near—that too you would have to accept. You loved it once, and although you've experienced the danger—well, life is dangerous, Joanna. Driving a car, flying, our own work, marriage, having children——' his face changed. 'Damn, I'd forgotten! Of course, there's Andrew!'

The sudden anxiety in his voice brought Joanna out of her trance like state. She shook her head vehemently.

'Andrew doesn't come into it. He means nothing to me. As for the rest——' She broke off and sat pondering while he waited in silence. His offer was so tempting and his commonsense attitude to her deep-seated fears was just what she needed to restore her to a normal frame of mind. After all, she told herself, she could always leave if things didn't work out. Paul would have no difficulty in finding another partner and she could easily find another job. At last she said carefully, 'It's a very attractive proposition, hard to resist. I'd like a little time to think it over.'

'Plenty of time,' he said cheerfully. 'I must give at least a month's notice to Mr Mayfield.'

For a few minutes longer they both remained silent. Then suddenly he turned to look in the back of the car and sighed heavily. Joanna twisted in her seat and followed his gaze, and it was then that she realised his old dog was lying stretched out, fast asleep.

Startled, she exclaimed, 'Good gracious! I'd no idea Ben was here. Surely he hasn't been in the car all day?'

'Of course not!' Paul said sharply. 'He's been with my sister. I put him in here when you went to wash your hands after playing with the puppies.' He paused and his voice trembled. 'I'm afraid he's come to the end of the road. No more joy in life—it's cruel to let him go on any longer. But I was hoping to give him one last pleasure. That was why I took this road to the coast. He's always loved a run along the beach—his favourite outing when I lived down here—and I never miss taking him when I come for a weekend. I very much want to take him for his last run now. Will you come with us?' He sighed again. 'Perhaps you think I'm being too sentimental?'

'No, you're not,' Joanna said quickly. 'I'd do the same in your place. But wouldn't you rather be alone with Ben?'

'No. I—' Paul hesitated, then said simply, 'I need

you.'

The old dog lifted his head and sniffed the salty air as they approached the sea, and when they helped him out of the car and on to the beach his tail wagged gently as though in joyful remembrance of his youth. For a short time he seemed to recover a little of those earlier years, running on a few yards and giving an occasional bark as small waves broke at his feet. The tide was going out, dragging gently backwards from the soft, wet sand, and to Joanna this sudden confrontation with the sea that had killed James and so nearly drowned her as well brought on a fit of trembling. Then suddenly Ben collapsed, unable to go any further, and all thoughts of the past vanished as Paul ran forward to pick him up. With misty eyes she saw him lift Ben into his arms as though he were still a puppy, and Ben looked up into his master's face and licked him gratefully. She followed in silence as he walked back to the car and, opening the door, she stood aside as Paul laid the dog on the back seat. She was about to get in herself when he said sharply,

'Wait! Not yet. I'm going to put him to sleep.'

'What, now? Here?' Aghast for a moment, she stared at him, then suddenly she recognised the compassion underneath his decision. 'You're right,' she said quietly, and turning, she walked away from the car and stood looking out to sea.

She heard the soft murmurs of farewell, heard Ben give a loving whimper in response, and then there was silence. Tears flowed unheeded down her cheeks as she waited, and at last, Paul came up behind her. Unable to look at him, she put out her hand and he grasped it tightly.

'Let's go down to the beach again,' he said.

The moon was shining now, its rays reflected on the water, and it was all so beautiful that Joanna turned quickly to glance at Paul. Without a word he took her in his arms and, reaching up, she touched his face gently with her hand. His cheeks were still damp with tears and, overcome with compassion, she spoke without thinking. 'Paul—darling Paul, don't take it so hard. I can't bear it. I love you so.'

He tensed and tightened his arms so fiercely that she gasped. 'What did you say?' he demanded, and when, aghast at her involuntary admission, she tried to turn her head away, he took her chin and forced her to look up at him. 'Joanna—' his voice trembled, 'say that again.'

'I can't—I shouldn't have——' Then she met his eyes, heard him say, 'Oh, my darling!' and his mouth came down on hers.

When at last they drew apart he looked at her so tenderly that her bones seemed to melt. Half laughing, half crying, she said, 'I've given myself away, haven't I?'

'Yes, thank God!' He kissed her hair. 'I never guessed—I never dared to hope—oh, Joanna, I love you so much! I don't think I'll ever be able to tell you how much, but when we're married——' His mouth twitched at the corner. 'I'm not asking you—I'm telling you—when we're married I'll spend the rest of my life trying to show what you mean to me.'

On their way back to the car Joanna turned and took a long look across the water. The ghost of James was laid at last. Exorcised by this wonderful night of moonlight and a whispering sea. A sea that had washed away the past and now spoke only of a future filled with love and happiness.

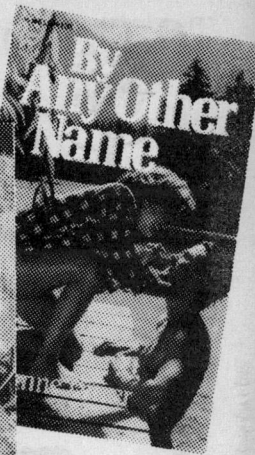

A WORLD WHERE PASSION AND DESIRE ARE FUSED

CRYSTAL FLAME — *Jayne Ann Krentz* _____ £2.95
He was fire — she was ice — together their passion was a crystal flame. An exceptional story entwining romance with the excitement of fantasy.

PINECONES AND ORCHIDS — *Suzanne Ellison* _____ £2.50
Tension and emotion lie just below the surface in this outstanding novel of love and loyalty.

BY ANY OTHER NAME — *Jeanne Triner* _____ £2.50
Money, charm, sophistication, Whitney had it all, so why return to her past? The mystery that surrounds her is revealed in this moving romance.

These three new titles will be out in bookshops from October 1988.

WORLDWIDE